The Navigator

The Navigator

A Medieval Odyssey

Screenplay by
Vincent Ward, Kely Lyons and Geoff Chapple
from an original idea by Vincent Ward

faber and faber
LONDON · BOSTON

First published in 1989
by Faber and Faber Limited
3 Queen Square London WC1N 3AU

Photoset by Wilmaset Birkenhead Wirral
Printed in Great Britain by
Richard Clay Ltd Bungay Suffolk
All rights reserved

© Vincent Ward, 1989
Foreword © Nick Roddick, 1989

*This book is sold subject to the condition that it shall not,
by way of trade or otherwise, be lent, resold, hired out
or otherwise circulated without the publisher's prior consent
in any form of binding or cover other than that in which
it is published and without a similar condition including this
condition being imposed on the subsequent purchaser.*

British Library Cataloguing in Publication Data is available.

ISBN 0-571-15443-3

Contents

Foreword by Nick Roddick	*page* vii
Introduction	xiii
The Navigator	1

Foreword

In early March 1984, I found myself sitting in a screening theatre at the New Zealand National Film Unit. It wasn't the best way to see a film. Only one reel had a full soundtrack (the rest just had dialogue, without music or effects). The print wasn't graded, and several of the crew were there to point out, not always in the most hushed of tones, the things that still needed to be done. Two hours later, a couple of things were clear. One, I no longer needed to apologize for what most of my friends regarded as a rather quaint interest in New Zealand films (some of them, I think, were convinced I was actually a closet Kiwi who had done a great job on his accent). And two, *Vigil* was the most extraordinary first feature I had ever seen.

Three months later, the film's director, Vincent Ward, came to stay with us in London after *Vigil* had been in competition in Cannes (where, incidentally, it had produced a fiercely divided response). He arrived with a rucksack, and proceeded to buy a large electronic typewriter. They made an interesting combination.

On the typewriter, he began to work at an idea about a group of medieval Cumbrian dwarfs who tunnel through to twentieth-century New Zealand. I wish I could say I thought it was a winner, and that I could see, as clearly from that germ of an idea as from the work print of his previous film, the brilliance of the final result. But I couldn't. Not that this bothered Ward, who continued to work on the idea that winter in New York, then back in New Zealand – though it was clear by then that he had very little interest in being part of the New Zealand film industry.

His interest was with what he wanted to say, and the New Zealand film industry didn't necessarily see that as its top priority. A new film industry is, after all, quite different from a new cinema. New cinemas arise, like those in France, Germany, Brazil and perhaps Britain, when the traditional ones have grown too comfortable and conservative. And a new film industry – and New Zealand's is, to all intents and purposes, even now only ten years old – is a crusading thing that breeds fierce commitments.

For a while, the commitment spreads across the board: financiers feel benevolent, or at any rate patriotic, especially if (as was the case in New Zealand) the government lends a hand with tax concessions; crews work unbelievable hours for (fairly) little money; and critics, who love to discover things, are (briefly) content to join in the celebrations. All that matters is that films are being made: C'mon guys, we can do it!

The problems start when the obvious stories have been told, the novelty has worn off, the financiers have found other, better tax dodges (in New Zealand's case it was kiwi-fruit farms and Broadway musicals) and the critics have reverted to type. By that stage – and that was the stage that had been reached when plans for making what would become *The Navigator* first began to take serious shape towards the end of 1985 – New Zealand's emergent film industry was, to use a graphic local colloquialism, pretty much stuffed.

The film, however, had to be made in New Zealand; so far, all Ward's films have drawn heavily on the landscape qualities of his native country. But Ward has otherwise pursued a course which is, at best, parallel to the rest of the New Zealand film industry. While Geoff Murphy was filming car stunts up and down both islands to make the country's first commercial success, *Goodbye, Pork Pie* in the late seventies, Ward, who had just finished art school, was making the sort of films that people who have just finished art school tend to make.

Then, as the Kiwi industry began to expand – the money, thanks to the tax breaks, was still available, and the rest of the world, for a while, was watching – he shunned the car chases and rural melodramas favoured by his peers for the fifty-five-minute *State of Siege* (1978), based on a novel by Janet Frame about a woman in an isolated house. A dark, brooding film, it is more about light and texture than it is about plot. But it was a crucial thing for Ward to make when he did, because it imposed the disciplines of working with a story and working with actors. It was time, he decided, that he tackled those challenges.

Ward is someone who thinks through the process of film-making more than any other director I have ever met. Somehow, though, the questions do not seem to pose themselves to him in quite the same way as they do to other film-makers. Like Martin in

The Navigator delightedly exploring the properties of the piece of No. 8 wire, Ward has an artisan's respect for his raw material (which sets him apart from his avant-garde beginnings) but refuses to accept that it won't bend any way he wants it to. Increasingly, the result of this thinking through has helped him carve out a style of film-making which is unique way beyond the context of New Zealand cinema.

The film in which it first really came together was a documentary, *In Spring One Plants Alone*, which won the Grand Prix at Cinéma du Réal in Paris in 1980. A forty-five-minute film about an old Maori woman living in an isolated, mud-soaked community, it mirrors the repetitive rituals of the woman's life in a formal film style all its own. Ward sets the shots up and lets the actions come into them – the exact opposite of tagging along behind them with a mobile camera. He has, through weeks of simply watching, become so familiar with what the 82-year-old woman does, day in, day out, that he can anticipate her actions precisely. The resulting film links a strong stylistic (and therefore artificial) concern to a series of evidently real actions without betraying either. Like all Ward's films, making it was clearly an obsessive process. Watching it is, as a result, a compulsive one.

With Ward's two features, the obsessiveness begins with the script and ends with the final mix. He reckons he drove 16,000 miles before he found the valley he wanted for *Vigil*, and that he looked at between five and six thousand schoolgirls before casting Fiona Kay in the lead. Even by those standards, though, the setting up of *The Navigator* was a marathon. What is more, it is perfectly clear that, if Ward and his producer, John Maynard, had not been obsessive about it, the film would never have been made.

The problems, as is nearly always the case with independent films, were not creative or even logistical; they were financial. Standing apart from the rest of the New Zealand film industry didn't prevent Ward from getting stuffed along with everyone else when that industry all but collapsed in 1986.

Making films is never easy, but it is rarely as hard as it was with *The Navigator*. Not at first, though; with the international critical success of *Vigil* behind them, Ward and Maynard looked all set to move swiftly on to the next project. An impressive slate of international pre-sales (financial commitments from foreign distributors without which very few films are made these days) was racked up and that, combined with the New Zealand Film Commission's biggest ever commitment to a single film, put *The Navigator* on course to be made in July 1986, three years after *Vigil* had been shot. July is mid-winter in New Zealand, and climate – more properly the elements – play an important part in Ward's films. So the room for manoeuvre was limited; if the film didn't start by a certain date, it wouldn't start at all.

The final slice of the budget proved more and more elusive, however, until with half the sets built and a cast and crew assembled, the plug had to be pulled on the whole project days before shooting was due to begin, letting a lot of money (not to mention dreams) run down the plug-hole. There were loud recriminations at the time, with Maynard accusing New Zealand investors of failing to back one of the country's most promising cultural exports. He was right, of course; more concerned (as, I am sure they would argue, is only right) with profit than promise, the potential investors ended up putting their money (NZ$10 million – over twice *The Navigator*'s total budget) into a Broadway musical instead.

With the project necessarily on ice for another year, Maynard and Ward moved to Sydney, in the hope of setting it up there. Finally, they succeeded. And, though the film was eventually made in New Zealand, it was the first Australian-New Zealand co-production, with funding from the Film Commissions of both countries as well as from private sources. Nor could it be made in Wellington, the city around which it was written, so that the very specific juxtapositions built into the original script – hillside, motorway, railway line, harbour, cathedral – no longer existed; the atmosphere and topography of Auckland (where the modern parts of the film were shot) are quite different to those of Wellington.

The vision of the film, however, survives (as it would doubtless have survived a transition to Sydney or, for that matter, Singapore). And it is the vision of the film – the interplay between images and ideas, and the dramatic tension that interplay creates – that determines its achievement, solving any lingering doubts left after *Vigil* that Ward, at 33, is a major-league film director.

In the end, too, for all that he may deny it, he belongs to New

Zealand cinema. Only in a new industry would a first feature as unique as *Vigil* have been made. And, without the experience of growing up in what Ward calls 'a culture that's very isolated, at the bottom of the world', the vision which became *The Navigator* would never have had quite those elements of sharpness and strangeness, of intense practicality (see, for instance, the scene in which the spike is cast) and intense peculiarity, like the horse in the boat.

Parallels with the work of other, established directors are obvious – bizarre details break through the studiedly realistic surface of Fellini's early films, too; the dark imaginings of Bergman's middle period have a similarly rigorous set of rules; and quests are undertaken almost for their own sake in many of John Boorman's films. But that doesn't mean that there are influences in Ward's work, and there are certainly none of those *hommages* that pepper the work of Ward's European contemporaries. His films are, intensely and uniquely, his own. But, in a strange and contradictory way, they are very much New Zealand's too; it's not just in his films, but on them as well, that a sense of place exerts itself.

Nick Roddick

Introduction

The Navigator is essentially about an act of faith – people believing they can change the course of their life.

Some historians have likened the fourteenth century to the twentieth century. They were both calamitous ages. The fourteenth century had plague, war and holocausts and this century has seen wars on vast scale and the potential for further holocaust.

I liked the parallel of the little, isolated village in Cumbria being a pocket skipped over by the plague, and of New Zealand, too, being a little pocket separate from the rest of the world. In both these cases, two small and isolated places have the belief that, to some degree, they can affect their own destiny – even though the odds seem against them. I believe faith and hope are prerequisites for action and change, regardless of the odds.

Basically what I wanted to do was to look at the twentieth century through medieval eyes. It's as if the demons of our contemporary world – our technological monsters of destruction – could be foreseen in the nightmares of medieval men. A dream of hell coming out of a medieval life that was bleak and colourless. By contrast, the twentieth century, as seen in a vision, would seem richer and more vivid. For this reason, I use colour to delineate the child's vision of the twentieth century, and black and white for medieval times.

To remind the viewer constantly that this is a medieval vision of the twentieth century, the twentieth century had to be portrayed in medieval colours. The blues used by the Limbourg brothers in the Duc de Berry's *Book of Hours* I used in the azure of roadside telephone boxes, police car lights and the moonlight grey-blue apparition of a nuclear submarine. Similar blues are those found in Chartres Cathedral (a blue it is said that glaziers have lost the art of making). This blue is contrasted with the fiery, hellish tones of Bosch, Brueghel and Grünewald. The fires of medieval torches – the sodium from the orange lights of the motorway and the burning gold of molten metal. Always, it's a world caught between the two spheres of the rising and setting sun – the time-frame medieval miners would relate to, as they would work literally from dawn to dusk; twelve hours in summer, ten in winter.

In medieval times, as always, the rich had the most powerful voice. Visionaries like Nostradamus – a doctor, well-off, élite, trained at the University of Paris – are remembered in history. But I liked the idea of giving a voice to the underprivileged – a nonentity, a mere child, from a tiny isolated pocket, unimportant in world events, but whose vision is pure and clear. No matter how valuable somebody's perception, coming from a lowly source would have ensured that it would be knowledge wasted, lost. In my first feature, *Vigil*, the central character was a twelve-year-old girl who invented her own realm of reality and lived through her imagination.

As we grow older and learn to rationalize the world, we often deny the richness of dreams, the importance of emotional adventure, the thrill of risk, and the vulnerability of courage. This new film centres around collective action, where a group of people protect something they love, where individuals fear a loss of courage in a situation where other people depend on them.

In a sense, the act of faith made by those who follow this child on his quest has a parallel in the making of the film. It was a very hard film to make and I was lucky to have a producer who made that act of faith, put himself on the line both professionally and personally and stuck to what proved to be a four-year task to make this film. It was this belief, and that of the cast and crew, which sustained this production.

Vincent Ward

The Navigator was shown as part of the Official Competition at the Cannes Film Festival on 18 May 1988. The cast includes:

GRIFFIN	Hamish McFarlane
CONNOR	Bruce Lyons
ARNO	Chris Haywood
SEARLE	Marshall Napier
ULF	Noel Appleby
MARTIN	Paul Livingston
LINNET	Sarah Pierse
Director of Photography	Geoffrey Simpson
Production Designer	Sally Campbell
Editor	John Scott
Music	Davood A. Tabrizi
Co-producer	Gary Hannam
Producer	John Maynard
Director	Vincent Ward

The Navigator was produced by Arenafilm and the Film Investment Corporation of New Zealand with the assistance of the Australian Film Commission and the New Zealand Film Commission.

Opening credits fade, followed by caption:
In the mid-fourteenth century, two-thirds of Europe's population succumbed to a new disease. The shadow which advanced across Europe, into England, was known as the Black Death.

LAKESIDE AND MOON. PRE-DAWN (*Black and white*)
Opening credits appear over a shot or shots of the moon and the lake . . . a figure, faceless, stands in the water.

LAKESIDE AND MOON. PRE-DAWN (*Black and white*)
The figure, knee deep in water, is weaving slightly. On the horizon in front of him the moon waxes almost full, shedding light on to the boy's face.
The moon seems to hold the nine-year-old GRIFFIN *in its glow . . . He dreams and dreams . . .*

THE DREAM. NIGHT (*Colour*)
GRIFFIN *is in a deep pit. He moves, flanked by five men, towards the edge of a wide fissure in the rock . . . there seems to be no bottom to it – it just goes down and down.* GRIFFIN *bends forward and hurls a burning torch over the edge.*

We see the same crevasse, only now GRIFFIN *helps the five men with their ropes lower a wooden machine.*

GRIFFIN *leads the small party of men on an underground expedition; they are tunnelling as they go with the primitive digging machine. Several times they look nervously back over their shoulders, as if fearing pursuit . . .*

It is night. Holding the burning torch, GRIFFIN *and the party of men look out from the tunnel over what seems to be a constellation of stars but which is in fact a vast luminous city. They are separated from it by the sea.*

On this sea beneath a full moon, a glistening black shape, a sea beast, submerges into the water. Beyond it the city skyline is partially revealed and as the beast sinks, the spear thrust of a cathedral soars into view. The medievals, now in a small boat, paddle furiously towards it.

The cathedral spire comes closer – a long metal pinnacle, a spike, is being hoisted to the very apex of the spire. (Note: it is a spire outlined by the full moon.)

A figure in silhouette climbs the final few feet up the spire precariously, clearly in danger of slipping. With one hand the figure climbs the rope, helping himself along painstakingly, hand over hand, one hand gloved, the other not . . .
Someone calls out in alarm.
SEARLE, MARTIN, ARNO *and* GRIFFIN *race towards the cathedral.*

Footsteps – feet race up the cathedral stairwell . . .

On the spire the spike is swung closer to its final position. It is inches away, the silhouette beside it straining to set it in place . . . as the feet are racing, racing to make it up the final part of the tower stairs . . .
The cathedral bell tolls once . . .

A face flattened and distorted by the force of a fierce wind, a face that is anguished and clinging to something, screams . . .
The cathedral bell tolls a second time . . . as the feet are racing, racing to make it up the final part of the tower stairs . . .
The figure on the steeple apex cries out, striving to swing the spike on to its base . . . again the feet, racing up the stairs . . . as the bell chimes one third and final time . . .

We see the distorted face screaming, screaming . . . but also moving at great speed – we can also see landscape, water, bushes, shooting by in the background . . . the moonlit water dancing . . .

The figure on the spire loses his footing, slips and starts to slide – but the pinnacle is in place.
The spike rides majestically high and in perfect position. The crowd is cheering.
Dawn breaks, strangely brilliant blue . . .

At the tunnel entrance villagers celebrate.
The moon, luminous, appears swollen in the sky.

Water . . . the lake. In the pre-dawn a box is being propelled through the water. It's a coffin, sealed, being pushed through the current . . . A string with something bright and shiny trails behind it in the water, and the figure who pushes the coffin is in silhouette, the water up to his waist . . . the dream ends.

THE LAKE. PRE-DAWN (*Black and white*)

There is a sharp splash as GRIFFIN'*s eyes start to open. Two of his sisters and his younger brother* LITTLE TOG, *stand laughing on the bank – they've splashed him to wake him up.*
GRIFFIN: (*Looking around/shaken*) (What did I. . . ?)
  (*The experience has been so intense that he can't get the words out.*)
ESME: (*One of his sisters*) We called you and splashed you and still you didn't wake. . . !
  (*Griffin's sister-in-law,* LINNET, *is watching from the brow of a nearby hill. She is over eight months pregnant.*)
LINNET: (*Calling*) Griffin! That's the fourth time this week!
GRIFFIN: (*Still clearly shaken*) It's the same every time – the cathedral, and people digging in the earth.
ESME: (*Warningly*) Oh, Griffin –
GRIFFIN: No – it's true . . . and there was a big fish – evil – queenfish. I remember . . .
LITTLE TOG: (*Bouncing around in a funny little dance*) It's true. It's true. It's true. It's true – Our Griff gets out of bed with angels in his head . . .
  (LITTLE TOG *chortles at his cleverness.*)

THE VILLAGE AND GAP. DAWN (*Black and white*)

GRIFFIN *grimaces and heads, slightly disoriented, towards the village.*

THE HOUSE. DAWN (*Black and white*)

The household is up, the room congested. GRIFFIN *makes his way through the kitchen area, where his grandparents sit near the hearth.*

His GRANDMOTHER *clucks at him – he ducks by her.*
LINNET *is listening to the two old people as she prepares food over the fire. She hoists a pot on to the hearth.*
GRANDFATHER: No, it was the omens first – when did they start?
GRANDMOTHER: (*Nodding, nodding*) I'm talking about the pedlar who was here on Monday last – find a lump under your arm at breakfast and you're dead by lunchtime he said . . .
LINNET: (*Leans back away from the fire*) It's Connor I'm worried about. If something is abroad . . . why isn't he back yet? It's been too long . . .
(GRIFFIN, *dressing in the corner behind her, listens to all this with a precocious worry in his eyes.*)
GRIFFIN: (*Resolved*) I'll find him . . . Tomorrow I'll go.
LINNET: (*Somewhat preoccupied*) The thought of him out there, and us not knowing . . .
(*Then she looks at* GRIFFIN *as if realizing he's there for the first time.*)
Oh, Griffin, the sun's on the west wall. You're going to be late.
(*Still changing he races towards the door, almost slips over his* GRANDMOTHER *before being hauled to an abrupt halt.*)
GRANDFATHER: (*Leaning close to* GRIFFIN) Dreamers will be clothed in rags, Griffin!
(GRANDFATHER *squeezes the boy's wrist taut, lets go – and sends Griffin firing out of the door.*)

VILLAGE – OUTSIDE THE HUT. DAWN (*Black and white*)

We see that the village is small, set on barren, snow-covered terrain near a lake. The houses are crudely fashioned, impoverished and temporary looking.
GRIFFIN, *still stuffing in bits of clothing while other bits fall out, walks along dragging a hod (used for carrying ore). The village is waking up – smoke curls from the rooftops, and there are people moving about. A* LITTLE GIRL *Griffin's age is feeding chickens in a yard. She looks quickly, sees him coming, then pretends she hasn't*

as he walks by with his head ducked, fully aware of her . . . he's almost past before they have the courage to sneak shy looks at one another . . . their eyes meet . . . she is brave enough to give him the tiniest smile before he hastens by . . .
Ahead of GRIFFIN, on the ground outside one of the huts, ULF is keeping a finial spike held steady atop the roof's gabled peak with a long forked stick while his brother SEARLE, sitting astride the ridgepole, hammers it into place.
It's an unusually tall finial spike. The other dwellings in the village have spikes as well, but none so large as this.
GRIFFIN slows as he passes, looking up.
GRIFFIN: Wasn't the one you had up there big enough?
(ULF turns and smiles. SEARLE doesn't, just keeps hammering.)
SEARLE: (To himself) Enough ill fortune's come down on this house for ten families since the new year began. If the sickness gets this far we'll need something to fend it off . . .
GRIFFIN: (Cheeky) You're lagging! Come on, bigfoot!
(ULF smiles at his freshness.)
SEARLE: (Between hammer blows) You be the bellwether boy, Griffin.
(ULF makes a sound like a sheep.)
ULF: Go on – we'll catch you up . . . we'll follow.

PITTED HILLSIDE AND VILLAGE. DAWN (*Black and white*)

Up on the rugged snowy hills above the village are the mining pits and slag heaps. Five fires are newly alight and burning, blown and fanned by three or four children who are already smutty from the work. Half-leaning on a tail-race which gushes water is a young ONE-LEGGED MAN. *He's filling a long chain of buckets, and someone else is carrying them to the five ore-washing piles near the fires. Even as the miners arrive the first hammers – rocks encased in a net at rope's end – are being swung by women to break up the ore.*

CAPTION: CUMBRIA, MARCH, 1348

GRIFFIN, SEARLE, ULF *and* MARTIN *head for the winch-lowered bucket which carries the pit workers down into the mine. They talk companionably as they go – men headed for a day's work* . . .

MARTIN: You remember the pedlar who brought you the faggots – he said – by the hundreds 'people falling dead without warning'.

SEARLE: I don't like it. Looks to be moving closer – we must trust in the spikes.

PIT TOPS. DAWN (*Black and white*)

The three men climb into the bucket, ready to descend, but CHRISSIE, *the winch operator, waits for* GRIFFIN.

GRIFFIN *has stopped, looking longingly over his shoulder, back down the road* . . .

SEARLE: (*Guessing right*) Come on – if Connor arrives old Chrissie'll let you know.

(*Old* CHRISSIE *smiles, straining against the brake.*)

CHRISSIE: Count on it, Griffin, and – well – Connor's sharp. He knows the ways of the world, and he'll be fine.

(GRIFFIN *reluctantly leaves his view of the open road, and hops into the bucket.* CHRISSIE *ruffles the boy's hair.*)

THE PIT INTERIOR. END OF DAY (*Black and white*)

SEARLE *and* MARTIN *are working against the vein of ore, already sweating from the labour.* ULF *is clearing the mined ore from the water around their feet, and piling it up some distance behind.*

GRIFFIN: (*Under his breath*) Connor . . .
  (SEARLE *looks over his shoulder at* GRIFFIN. *The boy is covertly notching a tunnel stanchion. There's a long series of notches, and* SEARLE *makes an easy guess.*)
SEARLE: So – how many days is he gone now?
GRIFFIN: Thirty-six.

A SNOWDRIFT AT THE BOTTOM OF A GULLY. SUNSET (*Black and white*)

Waist deep in snow, CONNOR *pushes through the drift. He looks driven. He uses his staff to pull himself forward . . . He stops suddenly to look over his shoulder.*

THE PIT. (*Black and white*)

GRIFFIN *stares at the notches.* SEARLE *puts his pick aside.*
SEARLE: Bear up, lad . . . and let's get you loaded up. It's work that drives away worry. And with the witches' spikes on our roofs we'll all be protected – eh, Martin?
  (MARTIN *answers between swings of his pick.*)
MARTIN: Oh, but the evil's too powerful, Searle. We need to go out – seek God's favour with a gift and . . . There's talk of places the plague just skips right over. An offering to God could make us safe. We'd become a pocket of safety – but we must take an offering to the right place first.
ULF: (*Dreaming*) An offering would mean a journey . . . wouldn't it, Searle? It'd mean . . . we'd take an offering to the big cities . . .
  (*He trails away into dream.* SEARLE *spins on him.*)
SEARLE: You!
ULF: . . . They'd draw back the curtain, and show us the holy relics . . . St Augustine's fingerbone . . . feathers from the Archangel Gabriel . . .
SEARLE: Ulf. You've never been outside the village before.
ULF: But none of us have.
SEARLE: (*Lowering his voice so* GRIFFIN *won't hear*) Nor wouldn't want to neither. Look at Connor, God spare him – still not back.

(*But* GRIFFIN *has heard. He shoots* SEARLE *a disturbed glance.*)
(*Whispering*) I wouldn't want to be in his shoes.
(*He is cut short by a shout from further up the mine.* GRIFFIN *is instantly alert. He hears old* CHRISSIE *distantly calling his name. He looks anxiously at* SEARLE, *who grins back his delight.*)
SEARLE: Go on –
(*Before anyone else can move,* GRIFFIN *scrambles around the ore mound, and is gone.*)
SEARLE: (*Laughing*) Hey – hold on!
(*Voices echo around the pit as* GRIFFIN *and the three men are hauled up past different levels of men working.*)
MINERS: Griffin – it's your brother!
Connor's back – !
Whoa there, youngster! Take care – you'll make it – !
Chrissie! Send word to the village – to Linnet and the family –
I told you – I said he'd be back – now we'll find out what's going on out there . . .

THE PIT TOPS AND THE ROAD. DUSK (*Black and white*)
The pit head is working fully now. Women, a few with babies strapped to their backs, are carrying ore from the mine to the smelting piles. Children carry pails of water, and armfuls of faggots. A BLIND WOMAN *is working a bellows with her foot. The* ONE-LEGGED MAN *is now stoking a fire. Women and old people are at work, breaking ore, washing it, smelting it roughly in the fires . . .*
GRIFFIN *bursts out of the pit-head, and looks . . .*
A figure approaches on the road, a wiry man, looking gaunt. He carries a staff and has a slight limp. His gait is hasty, as if he is pursued, and he keeps glancing back over his shoulder.
A dog bounds out to greet him, leaping with joy at his master's return.
GRIFFIN, *pelting down the road, spies the figure.* SEARLE, ULF *and* MARTIN *have reached the head of the pit . . .*
SEARLE *is smiling as he watches* GRIFFIN *run towards the distant figure –* CONNOR.
SEARLE: Look at him. You'd think they were married.
(*He laughs and waves. The figure waves back. Then glances*

again over his shoulder. GRIFFIN *runs along the road, shouting with excitement. The air is frosty – we can see the breath of both of them as they exhale sharply with their rapid movement.*
GRIFFIN *hits* CONNOR *full force, but* CONNOR *is ready for him. He catches him and lifts him into the air.*)
GRIFFIN: Con!
(*They're both grinning.*)
Tomorrow I was going to go out and find you!
CONNOR: (*Playing him along now*) And how would you've done that?
GRIFFIN: I would've flown like a bird. I'd've borrowed Black Jacob's horse!
CONNOR: (*Knowing* GRIFFIN's *pride is involved*) You would, eh? (*He swings* GRIFFIN *vigorously higher, then drops him carefully to the ground. He eyes him, then sweeps the stray strand of forelock out of the boy's eyes.*)
GRIFFIN: You'll not go away like that no more, Con – will you?
(CONNOR, *momentarily preoccupied, shakes his head. He's weary beyond words.*)
CONNOR: (*Quietly*) No, never . . . (*He jerks quickly back to the balm of his homecoming and drags a set of beads from his pocket.*) Look – it's a new method for counting your devotions.
(GRIFFIN *knows it's Connor's present, and makes a grab, but* CONNOR *dangles them high out of reach. He's not through yet.*)
They make them of oak for the great lords, and rosewood for the liege ladies . . .
(GRIFFIN's *jumping at them. He knows it's a game.*)
But this one's made from the hawthorn, Griffin – a scraggy tree, small and tough. (*He gathers the beads by a very non-religious clamping of his hand down on the suspended string.*) It reminded me of someone, Griffin.
(*He throws the beads to his delighted brother and leans towards him.*)
It's the tree they make axles from, Griffin. Axlewood. If I'm the big wheel on the move, still it's you at my heart . . .
(*He looks up at the noisy approach of family.*)
You and Linnet . . .
(*He's cut off as he and* GRIFFIN *are engulfed in the joyous, noisy mob of their family – tremendous relief and enthusiasm at the*

sight of CONNOR, *everyone talking at once* . . .
For a moment, CONNOR *and his pregnant wife* LINNET *embrace. She whispers, her lips close to his ear.*)
LINNET: If you'd not come back . . . I can feel it growing . . . Connor, it's over eight months gone now . . . God! I don't know what I would have done without you if you'd not . . .
(CONNOR *quietens her.* LINNET *pulls back from the embrace and looks at him searchingly. The rest of the family crowds around.*)
The dog's nose started bleeding, and wouldn't stop – we took it for a bad sign – thought for sure you were lost.
(*One of the children takes* CONNOR'S *hand* . . . *the others crowd around happily* . . . CONNOR *is slightly stunned by the outpouring of warmth.*
MARTIN, SEARLE, *and* ULF *hurry towards the reunion, grinning.* CONNOR *catches sight of them over the heads of his family. He shouts.*)
CONNOR: Hey, Searle! Martin!
(*He looks down.* LITTLE TOG *is pulling his hand, and he hoists him on to his hip, turns again to his family.*)
It's so strange to see people – smiling!
SEARLE: (*Over*) Hey!
(CONNOR *seems momentarily haunted again. His head jerks towards the cry. He puts* LITTLE TOG *down, distracted.*
SEARLE, MARTIN, *and* ULF *break through the circle around* CONNOR *on the wings of a joyful reunion.* SEARLE'S *hand falls on* CONNOR'S *shoulder.*)
Con!
(CONNOR *jumps in reflex, then flashes a smile, starts to relax again.*)
MARTIN: What's happening out there, Con?
(CONNOR *looks at him. Beyond him.*)
We've heard the stories. We've got to do something yes? We could meet – tonight?
(CONNOR *says nothing.*)

THE SMELTING GROUND. DUSK/NIGHT (*Black and white*)

The moon rises, huge and swollen over the Cumbrian hills. The chimney of the smelter sends out gusts of sparks, and thin trails of molten metal flow down a sandy embankment in front of it. A big set of bellows is working, and its slow soft breath is clearly heard as Martin begins.

MARTIN: There's a powerful evil on the move – Connor has seen it.
(CONNOR's *face remains impassive. We hear* ARNO, *he has interrupted* MARTIN.)
ARNO: A week back, I ferried a monk across the lake. He spoke of a great church being built in the west – the highest in Christendom once it's done, he said . . . And pilgrims come from everywhere to bring timber for its construction. You make an offering there – you stop the plague –
(*As he listens to* ARNO's *speech,* CONNOR's *face is still impassive.*)
SEARLE: The church is too far. Beyond the further reaches of the earth I heard. Across the mountains, across seas, past horrors there aren't even names for –
ARNO: (*Interrupts*) But, Searle . . . We've got to go. There's pilgrims on every road!
SEARLE: No! We stand our ground. Put our faith in the spikes!
ARNO: Put our faith in the witches' spikes on our roofs? It's not enough!
(*The villagers go silent.* CHRISSIE *speaks out of the silence. In his fist he holds a Celtic cross.*)
CHRISSIE: We need to use our metal for the tallest spike of all. Make the journey and cast the spire for the great church. Use the village cross, the bronze cross embedded in a spike at the top of the cathedral. That'll stop the plague. What of that, Searle?
(SEARLE *is isolated. The village is immensely taken with the idea.*)
VILLAGER 1: Make the journey! Pierce the evil! Do it!
MARTIN: Then – plan the journey – like the pilgrims! And Connor will lead us!
ULF: (*To* SEARLE) We're free miners, Searle. We've got the right of expedition?
VILLAGER 2: Aye! It's our best chance. Show the faith!
CHRISSIE: Cumbrian copper! God's best for God's big church. Here's to taking it. (*Waving his arm*) To a journey!

MARTIN: With Connor to lead our party we'd do it. He knows the outside world better then anyone here – tell them, Connor.
(*In effect,* MARTIN *is putting the motion, and the village quietens. People swing their attention to* CONNOR, *realizing in the silence that he hasn't uttered a word so far.*)
CONNOR: I've seen the pilgrims, Martin. I've seen so many bodies that there was not enough of the living to bury the dead. I've seen monks refuse the rites to the dying and the mobs chase them from their abbeys. Is it these same monks that head west as pilgrims, Martin? There are people no more than animals. You can trust no one. Children begged me for food but I didn't dare go near them. They had black boils, under their armpits, the size of shillings and they pretended they didn't have plague! The churches are empty. The plague rides forward with each full moon. We have a month, maybe two, to be with the ones we love . . .
CHRISSIE: (*Dogged*) Two months . . . a small party, well equipped, could reach the great church in that time . . .
MARTIN: (*Eager*) We could do it! Reach the church, and raise a spike of Cumbrian copper. With you or Searle to lead our party, Con –
(ARNO *quietly leaves the meeting. Meanwhile* CONNOR *turns to* MARTIN.)
CONNOR: Then it's Searle must do it . . . for I tell you I'm sick of all the death.
(SEARLE *stares mutely ahead. There's an embarrassed stalemate.* SEARLE *won't budge, but the silence acknowledges* CONNOR'S *distraught state of mind too.* CONNOR'S *eyes are downcast. The spell is finally broken by a warning shout.*)
DISTANT VOICE: Looters!
(MARTIN *glances around to see if the danger is near – but for the moment they seem to be safe.*)
MARTIN: You're amongst friends now, Connor.
(SEARLE *comes up. He takes* CONNOR'S *shoulder in a rough and friendly but hurried way.*)
SEARLE: Con, c'mon – we better see what's doing.
(*As he cleaves a path through the crowd,* CONNOR *is left behind,* SEARLE *calls back over his shoulder.*)

Hey, Con . . . I never thought I'd see the day when you'd stay put.

SMELTER – ABOVE LAKE. NIGHT (*Black and white*)

SEARLE *continues on to the ridge. He can hear the distant sounds of fighting now. Hell for leather,* ARNO *bursts over the ridge towards them – excited. He's beckoning furiously with his good arm shouting and pointing . . .*
ARNO: On the lake! Pillagers!
    (SEARLE *strides forward. He reaches* ARNO.)
SEARLE: Are they armed?
    (ARNO *nods.*)

DISTANT VILLAGE. DUSK (*Black and white*)

Over the lip of the ridge is the lake, and on the far side of it, an angry mob is turning away a boatload of people . . .

SMELTER – ABOVE LAKE. DUSK (*Black and white*)

CONNOR *looks. He's haunted by it. He connects it with the plague. With* LINNET *helping him he joins* SEARLE, MARTIN, ARNO *and* GRIFFIN.
CONNOR: Not pillagers –
MARTIN: No. There's women and children on board. Whole families . . .
CONNOR: It's refugees from the east –

DISTANT VILLAGE. DUSK (*Black and white*)

Closer now, the villagers of Gosford are staving the boat away from their shore with long poles. Others hurl missiles, and some of the boat people are responding. Someone wades out with a torch, brandishing it. A sudden leap of flames silhouettes the mast of the refugee boat. It flares briefly as the black figures on board rush to quench the fire. They throw water across the furled sail. Another

tongue of flame bursts from the stern of the boat. On board the burning boat a WOMAN tears the flaming tunic from her chest. As she flings herself towards the water we see that her body is partially covered in enormous black buboes. Now we see that the faces around her are similarly covered in obscene welts. The refugees like those around them are pushed, by the distant villagers, at spear's point deeper into the water. Laden down with clothing, unable to swim, frozen with cold, in some cases clinging to floating animals and other flotsam, they struggle in vain to save themselves from drowning.

SMELTER – ABOVE LAKE. NIGHT (*Black and white*)

CONNOR: . . . They're scared – scared of the death . . . we best keep guard ourselves.
(*Fade to black.*)

HILL (ABOVE LAKE). NIGHT (*Black and white*)
Fade up.
MARTIN, ARNO, GRIFFIN, SEARLE *and* CONNOR, *armed with*

spears stand guard overlooking the lake.
ARNO: (*Casual*) There is a story I heard once. About one of them old pits up behind the mines. There's supposed to be a hole so deep that if you dropped a stone down it, sooner or later it'd fall out the far side of the earth.
MARTIN: (*Excited*) The copper, an offering – we've got to take the offering, Con, to the great cathedral, to the far side of the earth.
(GRIFFIN *is having a strong sense of* déja vu *as they both speak. There's a brief silence, but when* GRIFFIN *speaks, his voice makes the others jump.*)
GRIFFIN: It's from the dream!
(*They all turn to look at him . . . A bell tolls in the distance.*)
SEARLE: Dream?
(GRIFFIN *nods. He remembers more and more clearly as he speaks.*)
GRIFFIN: In my dream we were tunnelling . . . through to the farthest part of the earth . . . We reached the cathedral and placed the spike.
(*They exchange glances in reaction to* GRIFFIN'*s story. They're earnest and become optimistic. The bell tolls again.*)
SEARLE: (*Good-heartedly*) Shite, Griffin!
(SEARLE *stops, his mouth open. The others turn to follow his gaze across the lake. Across the lake, distant villagers push coffins out into the water – small coffins pushed out past the burning refugee boat. There's lament and the insistent ringing of bells.*)
CONNOR: It's too late. It'll have hopped twenty miles on from Gosford by morning. It's the full moon bears the contagion forward, like a sack. At sunrise she lets it fall . . . on us!
GRIFFIN: Then . . . the journey?
ULF: I'll go!
SEARLE: (*Awed*) Ulf – no.
ARNO: Together.
GRIFFIN: A journey!
MARTIN: The pit's close enough . . . It's a chance. We could save the village.
GRIFFIN: Help me!
(GRIFFIN *sways slightly, his eyes out of focus. They all turn to him. Clouds black the moon. The boy crashes to the ground falling*

across some brushwood.)
LINNET: Griffin . . . what is it, Griffin?
(*The boy sways slightly. His eyes are distant as he begins to dream.*)

THE DREAM. (*Colour*)
We see figures with a primitive digging device burrowing. . .

We see the cathedral spire and the figure climbing it. . .

Water . . . the lake. A box is being propelled through the water. It's a coffin, sealed, being pushed into the current. . .

Again, burrowing figures with the digging device. . .

HILL (ABOVE LAKE). NIGHT (*Black and white*)
LINNET *is shaking* GRIFFIN *gently.*
LINNET: Griffin – what's wrong?
GRIFFIN: Nothing . . . the same . . . the pit.
SEARLE: Your head in the clouds again, Griffin!
LINNET: (*Flaring*) Leave him! There's signs within dreams – He's been right before – the blight on last year's corn. . . ? The vein of copper at the pit. . . ? Have you forgotten?
(*She looks across at* CONNOR – *anxious.* CONNOR *holds her gaze a moment, then turns to the others.*)
CONNOR: (*Reluctantly*) I'm with you – It's our only chance.
(*He takes the torch.*)
MARTIN: (*Delighted*) Con!
CONNOR: And Griffin comes too! Searle?
SEARLE: You're all daft!

CONNOR: You've got a better way then?
(*Clearly Searle hasn't. He shrugs.*)
We'd better see it.
(*He holds up his torch to Searle. The torch flames up in the darkness.*)

BESIDE A HUT (IN VILLAGE). NIGHT (*Black and white*)
ARNO: God! It's always me that carries the weight!
(*He stuffs the bronze cross into his pack.* CONNOR *is being strapped into his pack and equipment, while* GRIFFIN *stands nearby. The two are surrounded and attended by their large family.* MARTIN *and* ARNO *have five or six attendant villagers too, helping them settle their equipment.* SEARLE *is putting his pack on, alone, standing out to one side.*)
SEARLE: Where's Ulf? Ulf?

GRAVEYARD (ABOVE LAKE). NIGHT (*Black and white*)
It's a small rudimentary graveyard, ULF *is kneeling, talking to his mother's gravestone. He has a small cloth-wrapped parcel, and he pats it tenderly as he talks.*
ULF: There's a church in the far reaches of the earth, Mother. The greatest in the world. Pilgrims take gifts there and . . . that's the place for the little Virgin.
(*He smiles at the grave.*)
Why, God willing, I'll put her there myself. For you, Mother . . .
(*He smiles at the grave again, and leans forward to kiss the stone.* SEARLE's *voice makes him start.*)
SEARLE: (*Over*) Ulf!
(ULF *hurriedly kisses the stone and scrambles to his feet.*)

THE VILLAGE. NIGHT (*Black and white*)
The party is moving off. CONNOR *and* GRIFFIN, *together with* MARTIN *and* ARNO, *have a solid phalanx of people running beside them, patting them on the backs, waving, but* SEARLE *has no family. Again, he is obviously the loner as he stands to one side,*

calling and gesturing ULF *to hurry.*
SEARLE: Ulf! Come on, come on! (*The arm drops . . . He turns to follow the others, shaking his head.*) Always too far in front, or too far behind.
(*He starts off after the others, decisively settling a huge pack on to his shoulders.* ULF *runs after him, catching up at a shambling run.*)
ARNO: (*Calling out*) To the pit!

THE ABANDONED PIT. NIGHT (*Black and white*)
CONNOR: (*Quiet*) What is it?
GRIFFIN: (*Hesitates*) It's what I told you before . . . We're tunnelling through the earth, all of us, and we're using an engine. The engine's got a shaft, for breaking the rock and

dirt. It's the engine, you see, that makes us go fast enough to be there before the moon turns full.
(SEARLE *is staring at him, smiling slightly.*)
SEARLE: (*Good-humoured*) The moon's struck you daft.
GRIFFIN: No, it's true – I saw it in the dream, and I keep seeing it. And I'm sure that big black hole is there too.
(SEARLE *gives a little laugh, but he's interrupted by a shout.*
MARTIN *has gone ahead, around a bend. He's calling them excitedly. They follow the sound of his voice, which echoes oddly in the strange silence.*
GRIFFIN'S *head juts over the edge, wanting to know what's going on.*
MARTIN *has found the fissure . . . and something else. Their torches illuminate some sort of machine, sitting in an indentation next to the fissure.*
There's a small fall of shale at the back of the pit. SEARLE *and* CONNOR *both turn to look at* GRIFFIN.
GRIFFIN *moves slowly towards them.*)
CONNOR: What the hell. . . ?
SEARLE: I think you've got us all sleepwalking, old son . . .
GRIFFIN: But I've . . . I've never been down here before – you know that, Con –
CONNOR: (*Thoughtfully*) So . . . it's just like in your dream . . .
(GRIFFIN *nods.* CONNOR *picks up a large stone. When he casts it into the fissure they all lean forward silently, listening for it to hit . . . but there is no sound . . . only the updraught of wind from the crevasses licking at* GRIFFIN'S *toes.*
CONNOR *looks at* GRIFFIN *for explanation.*
Pause.)
GRIFFIN: We follow the torch – it's blown by the wind which comes from the other side of the earth. The wind blows through crevices too small for entrance, and we use the machine to tunnel.

WALLS OF CREVASSES. NIGHT (*Colour*)

WHHHOWWW!
The torch lights up facets of rock as it descends.

THE VISION – TUNNELLING (*Colour*)

The miners are tunnelling through the earth with the ancient machine. GRIFFIN *is in the lead, carrying a torch to guide them.*
PppsscchSCCCHHOOK!
The taut arm of the resurrected machine, released, smashes into the rock face ahead of them. There's recoil and shudder, dust and debris, then winding and the clank of chains.
WWWHHOOOOORRK.
The men duck as a huge rasp of breath from the bellows blows the rubble back behind them. As the dust clears the men's voices have a real sense of urgency to them . . . strained, choking on the dust, harried.
ARNO: Back up, back up – !
CONNOR: What is it – ?
ARNO: It's too dense here, too dense! Shift a bit – we're slowing up!
CONNOR: Keep it going – keep it going!

THE VISION – TUNNEL AND EARTH'S SHAPE. NIGHT (*Colour*)

The camera pulls back until we can see the shape of the earth far above them, and then the sky, where the moon is full, and clouds race across.

THE VISION – TUNNELLING. NIGHT (*Colour*)

Back beneath the earth . . . they strain and scramble to dig faster and faster.
SEARLE: We can't do it – the earth's too dense!
CONNOR: But we've got to – we've got to get there or we're lost – the village is lost –
(*There is a terrible unearthly scream that almost seems part of the imagined wind above. The sound fills the men with terror.*
MARTIN *claps his hands to his ears. He shouts!*)
MARTIN: Dig! Drill! We must keep moving faster than the moon!
GRIFFIN: It's not yet rising on the underside – but hurry! We can't slacken!
SEARLE: Then heave! Push! Turn the screw . . .

THE ABANDONED PIT. NIGHT (*Black and white*)

Back in the pit they're all focused on Griffin, fully concentrated, trying to understand, seeing something in this child they couldn't realize before.

ULF: But, Griffin, you'd fall straight out the underside of the earth after just two days' digging. Into the sky! Or you'd have to cling like a tick.
(*Pause.* GRIFFIN *hesitates . . . then he begins to speak.*)
GRIFFIN: It was further than we'd thought. Three times the length of your rope Arno – no . . . all of six times that length, before we struck the last hard rock between us . . . and the far side of the world . . .

THE VISION. (*Colour*)

The digging machine is angled sharply upwards now, and the miners brace it with their shoulders.
PppsscchSCCCHHOOK! It blasts into the wall, bucking, grinding. A number of little waterspouts gush from the wall, then . . . sssccCCHHPOOOOK! The machine breaks through in a burst of noise and rubble.
ARNO: Hell-bent for sunrise!!

THE VISION. (*Colour*)

(*When the dust settles,* GRIFFIN *and the miners are standing within a series of underground structures. They look around, a bit stunned . . .*)
SEARLE: (*Slowly*) What is it?
ARNO: (*Sniffs the air*) My God.
(*Pause. They've now all noticed the smell. Something is dawning on* CONNOR.)
CONNOR: It's tunnels, tunnels for the nightsoil. Only the great cities have them – underground sewers, where every household can empty its bucket.
SEARLE: It's huge . . .
MARTIN: (*Thoughtful*) Whatever civilization is up there must be . . . vast.

CONNOR: Look.
  (*In a recess in a wall some twenty metres away, a slender metal ladder ascends in a pale shaft of light.*)
GRIFFIN: (*Piping up out of nowhere*) I'll go.
  (*They turn to look at him, but he's already making his way over to the ladder.*)
CONNOR: (*Concerned*) Wait a minute –
GRIFFIN: No, it's all right – I'll be able to tell where we are.
  (CONNOR *can't argue with this logic, but it doesn't allay his worry.*
  They help him prepare. ULF *ties a rope around his waist.*)
ULF: . . . just to be safe – you never know . . . (*Shyly whispering*) about falling off, I mean . . .
CONNOR: Yer air bladder, Griffin.
  (*He reaches over and adjusts the pig's bladder around* GRIFFIN'S *neck.*)
  (*Adjusting the nozzle*) Here – till we find out if the air is poisonous or full of the contagion.
  (GRIFFIN *is outfitted, ready to go.* CONNOR *reaches forward and flicks the forelock from the boy's eyes.*)
  Godspeed . . .

(*A steady moment, and then* GRIFFIN *moves off. He looks like a medieval cosmonaut as he ascends. He disappears.*
The other five wait at the bottom. They're straining upwards for any sound, any hint of danger. MARTIN *looks down at his feet a moment. He gives a little surreptitious hunched jump.*
Then GRIFFIN's *voice echoes down, hollow with wonder.*)
GRIFFIN: I can see it! The city! The city's like – like – like stars – like – all the stars at once –
(CONNOR *whacks a hand into his palm.*)
CONNOR: We're here!!!
(*He claps his hands together, and raises them above his head in triumph.*
Everyone's bursting, laughing, talking, slapping each other on the back, gripping each other's arms.
One man at a time they start up the ladder, staying close together. ULF *starts up ahead of* SEARLE, *who is the last to come. As* SEARLE *puts his foot on the bottom rung* ULF *turns around uncertainly, looking back at him.*)
ULF: Searle . . . I'm afraid . . .
(SEARLE *grips his ankle reassuringly.*)
SEARLE: It's all right, good brother (*Smiles.*) . . . Come on.
(SEARLE *nods assurance to the question in* ULF's *eyes, and* ULF *turns and starts up the ladder.*)

FOOTHILLS. DUSK (*Colour*)
ULF's *head pops up out of the hole. His face goes smooth with amazement at what he sees. For a moment he looks extremely young.*
CONNOR, GRIFFIN, MARTIN *and* ARNO *are standing in front of him, looking out at what he sees.*
ULF: (*The sound escaping involuntarily*) Oh-h-h . . .
(*A peacock struts past his field of view and . . . In the low distance, across a body of water, a city lies spread out over low hills. It sparkles and glows with light in the approaching dusk. They stand staring, amazed at the size and brightness of the city.*)
ARNO: It's like it's on fire – ! A hundred thousand fires and torches.
MARTIN: Think how much tallow you'd need for all that.
(*Pause.*)

GRIFFIN: That's the city. The one I've been seeing in my dreams.
MARTIN: Lights . . . water . . . trees . . . grass, and . . . (*He gives a very tentative hunched jump.*) . . . something sticks it all to the earth. (*He solves the problem – weighing it in his two hands.*) God's goodness! It makes sense! Anything flat's got two sides, and if the evil was our side then surely God's goodness is –
(*He peers out again.*)
It'll be God's city all right. Can you see his great church?
(GRIFFIN *stares hard, but shakes his head.* SEARLE *is puzzled by this.*)
SEARLE: No. . . ? What do you mean. . . ?
GRIFFIN: I can't see it. . . ?
SEARLE: I don't like it . . . nothing's higher than a church spire . . . surely you'd see it?
(GRIFFIN *shrugs uncertainly.*)
CONNOR: Searle. In the big cities battlements are higher than a man can see over.
SEARLE: But the boy, Griffin – surely he must know where it is.
(SEARLE *looks dissatisfied. It is only because of* CONNOR's *authority that he is part way appeased.*)
CONNOR: C'mon, Searle.
(SEARLE *turns to* CONNOR.)
SEARLE: Well – just remember, Con. There's a run of ill-luck struck our family and . . . Ulf and I – we have to take care.
(*In the background* ULF *runs part way down the hill, arms flapping like a bird set for take-off.*)
MARTIN: But . . . it must be God's city! There's so much light.
SEARLE: Where's Ulf – Ulf!!
(ULF, *his arms levelling off for gliding, is clearly heading off in the wrong direction.*)
ULF: (*Exuberant*) I'm over here! Don't leave me behind!
CONNOR: If we're all to get there in time we go as the crow flies.
(ULF *bounding along behind them, has almost caught up.*)
ULF: I've always had to stay at home, you see, so I'm glad to get the chance to journey out a bit – you see, I've got something

special –
GRIFFIN: – a lady in wood . . .
ULF: – she was my secret . . .
   (ULF *cradles the small parcel under his arm. He looks up to* SEARLE *who has been watching, puzzled.*)
   (*Slightly defensive*) It's the little Virgin our mum gave us before she passed on. I'll put her in the cathedral for her myself. (*Glances at* GRIFFIN.) Can you see me placing her as an offering for Mother then?
GRIFFIN: Well . . . I'm sure it's just . . . I'm sure I'll keep remembering things as we go along, you know – any bits that are missing.
   (SEARLE *keeps silent. But it is clear from the coldness of his glance that he is disturbed.*
   CONNOR *too, looks strained. He is standing back now just slightly distanced from the others. And when he speaks, there's an edge of urgency.*)
CONNOR: Come on, Searle. Let's just get on with it.
   (*The others nod.*)

THE NEW WORLD – FOOTHILLS. DUSK (*Colour*)

ULF *bounds enthusiastically on ahead of the group – he has soon disappeared.*
CONNOR *stops, looking around to get his bearings – they can't see the city from where they stand.*
CONNOR: (*To* GRIFFIN) What do you think – ?
GRIFFIN: (*Slightly distracted*) It looks right . . .
   (SEARLE *glances around suddenly.*)
SEARLE: Where's Ulf? Where did he go?
   (*A cry from up ahead seems to confirm* SEARLE'*s alarm. After a second's hesitation the group runs towards the sound.*
   They break through a line of hedge and trees and pull up short.)

MOTORWAY. DUSK (*Colour*)

ULF *is happily walking across the first two lanes of a four-lane motorway, gesturing enthusiastically to them all. The road is empty.*
ULF: Come on . . . Come on!

(*A traffic light thirty metres away changes to green.* ULF *is caught standing just off the centre line . . . He freezes completely as the cars, trucks and buses roar by on either side of him, dangerously close.*
There's nothing the others can do but watch in fear.
Some of the vehicles blast their horns in warning as they race by . . . they seem to engulf him.)

SEARLE: (*Shouting in alarm*) This doesn't look like God's work to me!!
(*Suddenly the traffic slows to a trickle, then stops (the light has changed again). The miners erupt into shouts and orders which seem to have no effect on* ULF *until, in a series of awkward and spasmodic movements, he makes his way over to them with amazing speed, like a mad marionette.*
The traffic roars into life once more behind him.
He can't seem to speak. SEARLE *takes his arm as the group retreats to shelter. They peer out at the motorway.*)

ARNO: Well . . . we can't steer our course unless we get across that . . . somehow.
(CONNOR *looks at* GRIFFIN.)

GRIFFIN: (*Bothered, shaking his head*) I don't remember it . . . (*Pause.*)

CONNOR: We better cross . . .
(CONNOR *goes to the edge of the pavement. It's like jumping into frigid water – he looks back once, sets his jaw and goes.*
Immediately, the others, not wanting to be left behind, follow. Clearly none of them understands the principles of traffic flow.
CONNOR, MARTIN, ARNO *and* GRIFFIN *somehow succeed in getting across, although with difficulty.*
But the light has changed leaving SEARLE *and* ULF *cut off.*
SEARLE *remains stranded on the traffic island in the middle.*
ULF *quickly retreats back to the side he's come from. He has met his nemesis. He's so fragmented from his recent experience that he seems unable to set foot on the roadside even when it's empty. From the traffic island* SEARLE *encourages and cajoles him to the kerb's edge; but for each new attempt the light has already changed and* ULF *freezes in terror.*
It happens again and again, to the point where it becomes sad and comical all at the same time.

SEARLE *makes another try. Fully believing that this time* ULF *is about to follow, he leads off by example. He almost succeeds in getting across without being struck. A bus glances against his shoulder and sends him sprawling into the others. He picks himself up painfully, staring angrily in the direction of the distant vehicle. The traffic clears, and we see, outlined by blue light from a telephone kiosk, that* ULF *is still on the other side.*
SEARLE *and the rest urge and encourage* ULF *over the traffic's roar, but he just stands there, his parcel under his arm.* SEARLE *tries to go back, but the others stop him.)*

A WHILE LATER – MOTORWAY. NIGHT (*Colour*)
All attempts to get ULF *across have obviously failed. They sit or stand around disjointedly.* SEARLE *stares across at his brother.*
CONNOR *comes up behind him.*
CONNOR: Searle. (*Pause.*) We've got to go.
  (GRIFFIN *has joined them.*)
  The moon's already up.
SEARLE: (*Abrupt with despair*) We can't just *leave* him.
CONNOR: Listen to me. We've all got our tasks to do here – all of us. We can't abandon what we set out to do because one of

us isn't able to –
(SEARLE *jerks himself away from* CONNOR *violently.*)
SEARLE: (*Anger which can't help itself*) Yeh – right!! It's fine that it's *my* brother we're leaving behind, isn't it? Eh? You who don't give a bloody damn about anything except your God-forsaken wanderings all over Hell's half-kingdom – that's the top of *your* list, isn't it?! Then your family and everything else underneath *that* –
(CONNOR *stares straight at him, his face expressionless.*)
(*Pause.*)
CONNOR: (*Quiet and even*) You're wrong about that.
(*He turns away and begins to strap on his ropes and other equipment.*
GRIFFIN *hands him a piece of equipment. For no apparent reason,* CONNOR *flicks* GRIFFIN's *forelock out of the boy's eyes. Their eyes meet – in that instant there is uncertainty about* CONNOR, *something strained around the eyes.*)
(*Softly*) Godspeed, Griffin.
(GRIFFIN *half-smiles, but clearly doesn't comprehend* CONNOR's *intention.* CONNOR *turns back to* SEARLE, *adjusting his load in a decisive movement.*)
We separate here.
(SEARLE *and the others look at him, not understanding.*)
I'm going to go on to the cathedral (*Sees their questions.*) We'll never have time to rig the spire if we stay together. I can travel faster if I'm alone, and I can have the rigging done by the time you arrive.
SEARLE: But. . . ?
(CONNOR *gives a violent jerk to one of his shoulder straps.*)
CONNOR: It's Ulf – or the village, Searle! You take charge here! Find a foundry – get that spike cast – get it to the cathedral – Come on! Let's everyone do what they have to do.
(SEARLE *is now torn by another problem.* CONNOR's *departure.*)
SEARLE: Connor – no!
(SEARLE *fastens on to the most obvious difficulty in Connor's plan.*)
Take charge! Find a foundry! In this place?
CONNOR: All you have to do is use your nose. Even in the big cities you can smell out a foundry – gauge the wind – steer a

course –
(CONNOR *looks* SEARLE *right in the eye.*)
And you take care of the boy, Searle.
(SEARLE *looks at him.*)
GRIFFIN: (*Alarmed*) Connor – !
(*But* CONNOR *has already begun to move away.*)
Con, you promised . . . You swore you'd never leave.
(*He runs after his brother.*)
CONNOR: (*Under his breath but loud enough that* GRIFFIN *hears it clearly*) Stay away from me –
GRIFFIN: (*Running*) Wait!
(*But* CONNOR *shocks them all as he turns and strikes* GRIFFIN *across the face with his open hand. The blow is sufficient to stop* GRIFFIN *in his tracks. He reels backwards, stumbles, and sits down hard, catching himself with his hands.*
CONNOR *walks away swiftly. He swings himself across a fence and on to a track – a railway track. In a moment he is out of sight.*
They all stare after him. MARTIN *walks over to help* GRIFFIN *up. He sees blood.* GRIFFIN *has cut his hand on a piece of glass which glints up from the dirt.*
SEARLE *begins to shoulder his equipment.*)
SEARLE: All right. Let's make sure we get there on time.
(SEARLE *takes a few steps back towards the highway to stand staring at* ULF.
MARTIN *starts to bind* GRIFFIN's *cut hand with a rag.*)
GRIFFIN: Connor's gone! He could be lost and . . . the city's so big, Martin – so queer.
MARTIN: Don't fret, Griffin. He wants what's right for all of us, and however big the city, there's only one church.
(GRIFFIN *looks down at his bandaged hand.*)
GRIFFIN: And . . . he hit me!
(SEARLE *concentrates on* ULF.)
SEARLE: Ulf! Wait for me! I'll come back for you, I swear it! Do you hear me? We'll come by on our way back.
(*He looks for some kind of response, but* ULF, *his face baffled and sad, seems not to hear. His parcel is clutched tightly under his arm. His hand opens and closes on one corner of it rhythmically, in a very small movement. He gazes out over the traffic.*

SEARLE *turns slowly and walks away, looking back several times. As he hastens to catch up with the others, there are tears in his eyes, and as he rejoins the group* MARTIN *grips his shoulder sympathetically.)*

A SMALL HILL OVERLOOKING SEA AND CITY. NIGHT (*Colour*)

GRIFFIN *flexes his fingers, the makeshift bandage is uncomfortable. He is leaning forward over the hill's brow. He sniffs the air then turning to the others shakes his head.*
GRIFFIN: I think I knew about Ulf from the dream.
SEARLE: (*Tersely*) The direction, Griffin! The direction!
GRIFFIN: Nothing, nothing downwind of that direction . . . You'd smell the burning metal or the forge.
(*He turns in the other direction.*
GRIFFIN *leans forward. In the distance, near water, a chimney bellows smoke from a steel works.* SEARLE *looks to* GRIFFIN *searchingly.*
GRIFFIN, *like a scout, pauses, walks forward separating himself from the others, faces obliquely into the new direction, sniffs the air tentatively, then facing full on into the new direction sniffs the air with more assurance.*
His reply is more optimistic than sure – behind his back he crosses his fingers.)
Mmmmph – It must be . . . metal.
SEARLE: Right. We stay clear of the black highroads. We'll leave no one else left behind like – Ulf, stranded. We find the foundry, then we cross water. We go as the crow flies.

STREET – INDUSTRIAL ZONE. NIGHT (*Colour*)

SEARLE, GRIFFIN, MARTIN *and* ARNO *have moved further into a suburban industrial zone.*
GRIFFIN: I knew it . . . I knew it.
(SEARLE *turns in quick response.*)
SEARLE: (*Somewhat sharply*) What do you mean – ?
(GRIFFIN *is a bit uncertain in the face of* SEARLE's *sharpness, but he goes on.)*

GRIFFIN: I did know about Ulf – from the dream.
(*We see a brief flash of a segment of Griffin's dream.*)

THE DREAM. (*Colour*)
A face flattened and distorted by the force of a fierce wind is clinging to something and moving at great speed.

On the sea beneath a full moon, a glistening black shape, a sea beast, submerges into water; beyond it the city skyline is partially revealed. As the beast sinks, the spear thrust of the cathedral soars into view. The medievals, now in a small boat, paddle furiously towards it.

In slow motion, SEARLE, MARTIN, ARNO *and* GRIFFIN *start to race towards the cathedral.*

STREET – INDUSTRIAL ZONE. NIGHT (*Colour*)
SEARLE *has bent over to bring himself face to face with* GRIFFIN.
GRIFFIN: See – in the dream, I never saw Ulf reach the cathedral – all the rest of us, but not him.
(SEARLE *straightens up. Silence as he stares at* GRIFFIN. *We see a flash of* ULF – *forlorn – abandoned at the motorway. Then . . .*)
SEARLE: (*Firm, getting angry*) Griffin, if there are things in your dream that can help us, keep us out of danger, you've got to make sure we know about them. If we could have kept Ulf from walking into that –
(*He chokes up, almost cries again. The very thought that it could have been prevented is making him angry and apprehensive.*)
GRIFFIN: (*Quick, defensive*) But I didn't know! I can't know what everything means –
SEARLE: (*Sharper*) Well, if you *do* know about something, make bloody certain you warn us, that's all.

There's thirteen in your family and still growing. It's not the same for me and Ulf.

GRIFFIN: (*Indignant*) But I –

SEARLE: No arguments! Just stay alert, and tell us what you remember.

(SEARLE *and* GRIFFIN *are hurrying along a deserted industrial street. There's no sign of the concealed exit ahead, but you can hear a pick-up revving high, taking off.*

GRIFFIN *is bent right out of shape, running ahead of* SEARLE, *talking to himself fiercely.*)

GRIFFIN: Bastard! If Connor were here! If it weren't for you Connor would be here –

(*The pick-up bursts across* GRIFFIN's *path. He thumps noisily into the side of it and his cut hand leaves a streak of blood on the metal. He rebounds backwards and sits heavily on the ground. The pick-up slams to a halt. The side window shatters to smithereens as* SEARLE's *first ingot hits target.*

SEARLE *runs, reaching back into his pack for another ingot. He throws again and it whangs off the bonnet. The pick-up takes off with a squeal of tyres.*

Two foundrymen, TOM *and* SMITHY, *dart out of the foundry door.*)

SMITHY: Oh, Christ! Bloody Eric –

TOM: And the bastard didn't stop –

SMITHY: Hey – !

(SMITHY *puts a restraining hand on* TOM.

The medievals have reached GRIFFIN *and they're hauling him away from the foundrymen's approach. They're shooting anxious glances towards* TOM *and* SMITHY.

SMITHY *sees what's happening. His hand on* TOM *slows them to a walk.*)

TOM: Maoris?

SMITHY: Well – it looks like they've been in the bush awhile . . . The kid's all right.

(GRIFFIN *is on his feet. The medieval group is still backing slowly away before the foundrymen's slow advance, but now* GRIFFIN *is on his feet they seem to have forgotten to take him with them. He's free-standing between the two groups. His eyes are closed, his head tilted to catch a scent, and his injured hand*

comes up like a signal flag, pointing the way to the foundry.)
GRIFFIN: Smell it out – gauge the wind – Connor, I've got one.
(*The foundrymen reach* GRIFFIN. *The boy stands like a signpost while they look at his injured hand.*)
A foundry . . .
(SMITHY *examines* GRIFFIN's *hand. He works the wrist round in a circle.*)
SMITHY: Hurt?
GRIFFIN: A foundry . . .
(SMITHY *speaks almost idly while examining* GRIFFIN's *wrist and arm for broken bones.*)
SMITHY: Nothing broken. Don't worry, son, you're only the last in a long series of accidents – eh, Tom? We'll dress this inside the shop.
(SMITHY *brushes the boy's thatch of hair with his hand, reassuring him. By now the medievals have come right up close.* MARTIN's *nose is in the air, scenting.*)
SEARLE: Blacksmiths!!!
(TOM *looks back uncomprehending. He can't quite understand what the medievals are saying – their accent is too strong.*)

LATER INSIDE THE FOUNDRY. NIGHT (*Colour*)
ARNO *is leaning against the belt-driven grinding wheel fingering it questioningly.*
SMITHY *glances over at him warily then turns back to binding* GRIFFIN's *hand with a bandage. The two try to communicate with difficulty. Despite this it's clear that* SMITHY *feels an affection for the boy, perhaps he is reminded of his own grandson.* GRIFFIN *looks up at him enthusiastically.*
GRIFFIN: Blacksmiths! I knew it. I could tell by your smell.
SMITHY: I can't follow you, boy.
(*He smiles encouragingly down at Griffin, then looks over to* ARNO *who is hauling away at the grinding-wheel belt like a madman. Fat* BOB *starts to laugh, winks at* SMITHY, *indicates for* ARNO *to stand clear, then turns the machine on. As the machine starts,* ARNO *jumps back in surprise.*)
GRIFFIN: You're a smith?
SMITHY: (*Uncertainly, barely following his drift*) Aye – name's

Smithy.

GRIFFIN: Smithy, we've brought something for you to forge.
(SEARLE *nods his head impatiently.* SMITHY *shrugs, he's clearly still having difficulty with the accent.*)

SMITHY: You must be fresh off the boat, boy. I can't follow you. Now hold still . . . That's it . . . mmph . . . You're a brave lad.

TOM: They're not Irish?

SMITHY: No – Tom – give them a break – sound a bit like my grandfather – some sort of Scot.

SEARLE: Look, it's nearly midnight!! Our village will be done for!
(*He tears the pack off.*)
Copper! Cast it! Now!
(*He throws the contents of the pack on to the floor.* SMITHY *picks up a piece of the copper.*)

SMITHY: Copper – has some impurities, but pretty good – grade two.

SEARLE: You've got to cast it for us!
(SMITHY *looks around at the medievals sceptically. He is far from convinced.*)

SMITHY: Cast. . . ? You want us to cast the copper?!
(SEARLE *nods enthusiastically.*)

SEARLE: Yes – cast – yes!
(*He looks at* SMITHY *hopefully.* GRIFFIN *grasps* SMITHY'*s hand.*)

GRIFFIN: You've got to help us, Smithy.
(SMITHY *shrugs.*)

SMITHY: We're being closed down. I'm sorry, son.

GRIFFIN: You've got to help us. Go on! Please, Smithy.
(ARNO *has worked out how to use the grinding machine and it explodes with noise as he begins to grind the cross.*
It is then, suddenly, SMITHY *opens his mouth to speak. He stops then calls out to* ARNO *urgently. He has recognized the cross.*)

SMITHY: Hey – let me see that!
(ARNO *moves his hand away from the cross so that* SMITHY *can see it better.*)
How did you. . . ? That's our cross – Where did you – but we've never cast from that mould before – it's not cast . . .

Give it here.
(ARNO *backs away, holding it to himself.*)
Look. We're the only ones who own that mould. You can't have cast . . .
(*He reaches under some junk and pulls out the mould for it. Then taking the mould he closes in on* ARNO. *He puts his hand around* ARNO's *wrist and forces the cross into the mould – it fits exactly!* SMITHY *looks at the medievals – baffled, looking for an explanation.*)

GRIFFIN: It's for the spike at the top of the great church.

SEARLE: (*Interrupts*) We have to pour the finial with the village cross set at the very top.
(*He says it slowly so that the foundrymen will understand.*)

SMITHY: But that mould is from the old country. My old man's old man brought it here three generations back . . . and it was ancient then.

SEARLE: Pour the spike!
(SMITHY *looks at him blankly.*)
The finial.

TOM: . . . must be for the same church spire – but we were going to pour it two months ago. We've run out of money –
(*Crooks his thumb and finger into the shape of a coin.*) The Church hasn't paid us. The full casting bed's been stacked here for months while the church scratches around for enough money to buy the metal.
(MARTIN *is worried by the sound of this.*)

MARTIN: The church . . . is poor?

TOM: Well, just like any other business . . . if people don't like what you're selling.
(MARTIN *is boring in on this, he senses a mighty mystery.*)

MARTIN: Selling!!
(SMITHY *starts to laugh – they're all looking at him so earnestly* GRIFFIN *grabs* SMITHY *by the elbow and tugs at it urgently.*)

GRIFFIN: Pour the copper for us, Smithy! Pour the copper! Pour the copper!
(*Again* SMITHY *looks at the earnest faces, then down at* GRIFFIN. *He shakes his head and grins.*)

SMITHY: (*Sensing something*) From the old country, eh?

TOM: . . . and we thought you were the wreckers. Let's make it

our last pour, eh, Smithy?
(SMITHY *pauses, then makes the decision.*)
SMITHY: A pour it is, then.
(*Glowing metal falls in a molten rope from the crucible. It falls into a slag trough at the base of the spike mould.
The foundry is lit from this molten core. In the flaring and fading of light, the medievals are huddled together as though they're watching the game of their life.*
SEARLE *is grinning despite himself.* GRIFFIN's *eyes are as big as biscuits.* MARTIN *has a length of No. 8 wire in hand. He is watching the pour, but also, almost covertly, he keeps sneaking glances at the amazing properties of the metal in his hand. He bends it, straightens it.*)
BOB: Here! Give us a hand.
(SEARLE *starts – but he goes across, still grinning. With the help of the foundrymen, he grips a long lever, helps tip the crucible . . .*
GRIFFIN *looks back gratefully at* TOM *and* SMITHY. *It's as if he's been given all his Christmases at once.* SMITHY *half smiles and winks back at the boy. They're standing apart at the moment, watching. The light flickers on their faces.*)
TOM: You get it too, don't you?
SMITHY: Sure. They put the knife in . . . then someone gives it a twist.
TOM: Yeah. But what is it?
(SMITHY *is giving a roll-your-own a good hard smoking.*)
SMITHY: I think it's something we'd almost forgotten . . . love of the trade. It'd make you cry. The night they close us down is the night – I dunno – something comes along to show you how wonderful it could have been.
(*He throws the butt down as the two men start towards the pour. Three hot-metal channels lead from the slag trough, across the sand of the casting bed, to converge on the spike mould. But a hand-pulled sluice gate blocks any flow of the molten metal until the slag trough is full.
It's a simple enough job to start the flow-through though.*)
TOM: Over here – !
(MARTIN *arrives at the slag trough, and one of the foundrymen indicates a lever.* MARTIN *pulls it.*

Three incandescent rivulets of molten metal flare and smoke across the sand, converging on the base of the spike mould . . .
The spike suddenly exists, seven metres long, white hot, radiating light.
The spike again, just red-hot now and obviously cooling. The medievals are kneeling in front of it. MARTIN *is muttering a Latin incantation.*
    SEARLE *has regrouped the medievals. They come forward as a single force, all except* GRIFFIN, *who stands in front of* SMITHY. SMITHY's *hand rests paternally on his shoulder.*)

SEARLE: We'll waterbath the spike.
SMITHY: Nah! Just let her cool till tomorrow . . .
SEARLE: No –
GRIFFIN: (*Eager*) Before the dawn. We've got to raise it up by then . . .
TOM: Raise it!
    (SMITHY *knows enough about the medievals to speak slowly and to use hand gestures. He points first to the medievals, then to the spike which is still glowing.*)
SMITHY: You . . . want to raise . . . this . . . tonight?
SEARLE: Our man Connor's on his way to prepare the spire . . .
SMITHY: Tonight! You guys are fuckin' . . .
    (*He was going to say 'crazy' but the medievals are waiting for the foundrymen's agreement intently.*)
    . . . very fuckin' dedicated. But look – we owed you one right? Well – (*He wags a thumb at the spike.*) But raising it! I –
BOB: Let's help 'em put it up!
SMITHY: I –
BOB: Come on, Smithy – our last night. Give it a bash.
    (BOB *grabs a can of beer from behind him, rips the top off and hands it to* ARNO. *He does the same for himself – and swigs.*)
TOM: What d'you think, Smithy?
SMITHY: Well – who are you guys?
    (ARNO *is in mid-swig – aping* BOB.)
ARNO: (*Explosively*) Ale!
    (SMITHY *waves the question away. He recognizes instinctively the gap between them and him.*)

SMITHY: Never mind.
TOM: There's no money in this y'know. The church won't pay . . .
MARTIN: But – the copper is a tribute – And surely people have come, as we did, with gifts? From across the world.
SMITHY: Gifts!
(*He shakes his head. It's clear the medievals are again working a kind of spell on him. It's the effect of a simple strong loyalty, of simple verities. So that* SMITHY's *response is wry but gentle.*)
Well, put it this way. You'd probably be the first . . .
(TOM *wags a thumb first at the medievals then at himself.*)
TOM: The first and the last eh? What d'you say, Smithy – out with a bang?
(TOM *holds up a finger.*)
SMITHY: Raise it –
TOM: Right! Another hour and we can waterbath it. Then we'll sling some scaffolding into the wagon, ropes . . .
(SEARLE *is quick to organize.*)
SEARLE: Martin – you stay with the blacksmiths. But we'll press on – as the crow flies.
BOB: Well, not unless you swim. The cathedral's on the far side of the harbour.
(*Mention of the harbour sparks Griffin* . . .)
GRIFFIN: That's right! We cross water . . .

THE OCEAN. NIGHT (*Colour*)

The wide flat ocean is seen.
GRIFFIN *puts his hands up to his eyes as if to brush away water. He closes his eyes momentarily, and stares out unnaturally at the moon. He's seen a flash of dream and it disturbs him* . . .

THE DREAM (*Colour*)

A face flattened and distorted by the force of a fierce wind, a face that is anguished and clinging to something, screams . . . *It is* CONNOR. *He is moving at great speed – We see landscape, water, bushes, shooting by in the background. The cathedral bell tolls once . . .*

THE OCEAN. NIGHT (*Colour*)

GRIFFIN *shakes himself out of the dream. His fingers tighten around the rosary beads. He turns to the others.*

GRIFFIN: It's Connor. I think he's going to reach the church before us.

(ARNO *and* SEARLE *absorb this quietly. They've been rowing a small clinker-built boat. Aboard the boat is a horse and it wuffles in* ARNO's *ear.*)

ARNO: (*Unhappy*) Bloody horse! We should never have taken him. We'll never get there. We're too slow. The boat's too slow.

SEARLE: There's no way I was going by the black high road, Arno. You saw what happened to Ulf. You can swim back if you like, but I say again we stay travelling on the water!

(ARNO *flaps his mutilated arm at* SEARLE.)

ARNO: Swim back??!

(*He shakes his head unhappily. The horse nuzzles into the back of his neck then does a slobbering great lick all over* ARNO's *face.* ARNO *hisses back at it.*)

Yeah! It doesn't make any difference to you if I lose my other bloody hand for thieving.

SEARLE: Arno. The horse will be needed to winch up the spike.

ARNO: But you know what they did to me last time and all I did was borrow the cursed beast. It's thieving!

(*There's a shout from the shore. The horse's rider, in breeches and hard hat, comes limping along the beach, brushing away the sand from his fall. He waves his riding crop at them angrily and yells. Hastily* SEARLE *puts his back into rowing.*)

SEARLE: Arno – we've got God's own reasons – and that's enough.

(ARNO *is still jerking fearful glances over his shoulder in the direction of the shore . . . He hisses at* SEARLE.)

ARNO: If they take a hand for a horse, what the hell will they

take for a horse and a boat. . . ?
GRIFFIN: Sssshhh! There's something . . .

QUEENFISH SUBMARINE. NIGHT (*Colour*)
There is something large moving about out in the water. It has seen them and moves away . . . then closer. We see the medievals' dinghy from its point of view. The medievals are lit up against an old seven-foot buoy (a channel marker). They cannot see the presence watching them but rather sense it slipping through the water towards them. It makes a strange, unearthly noise . . .
ARNO: Strewth. God's eyes . . . (*Smiling nervously*)
Let's just take that horse back, shall we?
(SEARLE *is rowing full strength, but darting hard glances over his shoulder, hoping to outmanoeuvre the barely seen presence.*
The presence, some sort of giant fish, stalks them. It is circling closer. We see the medievals with their white horse and white boat from its point of view. They make a distinctive target. They're lit up by the moon, white against the inky black sea.
In fear the horse whinnies. For an instant its panicked snort of breath is caught in the cold light and its eyes flash. SEARLE *can hear the slap and see the swirl of water as the unseen fish moves still closer.*)
SEARLE: Arno. Take the oars. Keep us moving.
(SEARLE *ships the oars and scrambles to the bow beside* GRIFFIN. *He looks out to sea, then turns sharply on the boy.*)
Griffin! You didn't warn us! Huh! Griffin! I don't like this . . .
(*He turns to* ARNO *and sees that* ARNO *is making something with a spare oar at the back of the boat. They're therefore not moving forward.*)
I thought I told you to row.
(*He glares at* ARNO, *curses to himself and scrambles back to his rowing position under the horse.*)
ARNO: There's nothing out there, Searle. Is there?
(ARNO *chuckles nervously to himself.* SEARLE *barely acknowledges the question. He ships his oars in clumsy fear, his incomprehension surfacing in rage against* GRIFFIN.)
SEARLE: Where's your damn church, Griffin?! Is it the last

church in hell you're taking us to?!
(GRIFFIN *grits his teeth, blinks and stares into the darkness beyond them.*
Back at the stern ARNO *is expertly sculling the boat forward using a piece of leather wrapped around the middle of the oar as a rowlock, his foot to clamp the leather, and the stern as a fulcrum. From out in the darkness there is a shriek like a wounded bull.*
ARNO, *who is sculling hard, stops terrified. He can see the clear trail it now makes as some sort of fin cuts through the water while beneath it the bulk causes enormous upheaval and disturbance. The horse backs further into the stern of the boat, neighing several times, agitated and almost pushing* ARNO *off balance into the water.* ARNO *crosses himself at the thought.*
Again there is the moan of the beast, short and muffled, an answering echo to the horse's whinnies but deeper. The sea beast is making a circumnavigation of their position. We see them from its point of view – travelling fast towards them. The distance closing. Close on ARNO, *as the beast wheels towards him. Closer . . .*)
ARNO: Feed it the . . . Oh, God! It's judgement. It's come to get us! For stealing the horse! (*He takes the sins of the entire group on his shoulders. He turns once and screams at the apparition over his shoulder.*) We're sorry!!!
(*There is a sudden close, brisk burst of spray showering the medievals with water. The spout cascades thirty feet high and beneath it a glistening black fin and nose momentarily break the water's surface.*)
Jesus!!
(*It's gone almost as soon as seen. The water has changed all of a sudden to a darker hue. It is then they realize as they look out over the sides that an enormous dark shape is passing underneath their boat. It is more than thirty times their breadth and sixty times their length. It is Queenfish and its actual size can only be gauged from high above the dinghy.*
Mouth open, dumbfounded, SEARLE *stares down at the spreading shape, then frantically begins to row.*)
GRIFFIN: (*Disturbed, half remembering*) Queenfish . . .
SEARLE: You don't bloody tell us!
GRIFFIN: I didn't see it! How could I see that?
SEARLE: (*Muttering*) An omen. Seven angels and seven plagues.

A beast come out of the sea. An omen – an evil –
(*He pauses, thinking.*)
Then – it doesn't die . . .
(*The giant fish only now has passed fully beneath their boat. It is travelling fast.*)
ARNO: It's bigger than the whales! Bigger than anything I've ever seen.
(*The others stare silently, stunned by its size.*
It leaves in its wake a crest of water which smashes against the dinghy sending the medievals lunging for handholds and causing the horse to snort and trample. As SEARLE *grapples with the animal, trying to quieten its frantic lurching and splashing about, the boat is flung and thrown. The water washes into the boat and over them.*
SEARLE *has stilled the horse.* ARNO, *after regaining his balance, begins to bail furiously.*)
Oh, Mary, Mother of Christ. I can't swim. I can't swim, I can't swim . . .
(GRIFFIN's *head pops up from the bow. He surveys the wildly changing horizon for fresh sign of the threat.*
Further away a flick of foam marks the sea's surface indicating the sea beast's shifting position.
ARNO *looks up from bailing.*)
It's gone – scared it off. We're safe . . . I can't swim.
(*He laughs nervously.*
ARNO *is almost immediately answered. There is a sudden loud and enormous swirl of turbulence 100 yards behind them. It is easy to gauge the size of the turbulence as the channel marker they passed is immediately beside the swirl and* ARNO's *mouth drops.*)
It's turning! Oh God! We're done for!
(*Waves arc across the water towards them and slap against the dinghy's side.*)
SEARLE: Griffin! You didn't warn us!
GRIFFIN: It can't hurt us, Searle. We're on God's mission. Searle . . . we've the right of expedition!
(*Again we see the miners and their boat from the sea monster's point of view. The beast is far off but approaching. It sinks like a stone in a sudden swirl of eddies. Then from the depths the beast accelerates.*)

On the surface the water boils.
Then with enormous surge of noise and hiss from the up-lunge of water the black sea beast surfaces. Instant panic and confusion. The distinctive huge black shape of a nuclear submarine towers over them. Water washes hard against their bow, sending them flying in a confusion. The submarine relentlessly keeps approaching, a fin slices through their bow, smashing timber.)

ARNO: (*Desperate*) Harpoon it!
(GRIFFIN *seizes the opportunity without thinking. He hurls a bottle against the side of the submarine. It shatters, spraying glass over* SEARLE. *Too late he ducks. His glance back to* GRIFFIN *is full of misgiving.)*

GRIFFIN: Whale! Whale! Kill it! Kill it!
(SEARLE *is fully conscious of the second bottle even before it whizzes close past his shoulder and smashes against the side of the submarine. He flinches involuntarily then shoots a filthy glance in the boy's direction.* SEARLE *has been clinging to the side of the dinghy which has been pitched at a crazy angle and now realizing that it is better to fight than stay in his present position, he pokes at the submarine savagely with an oar.)*

ARNO: Spear it! Spear it!
(*Once, twice, three times* SEARLE *pokes at it – but each time the*

oar rebounds back towards him almost somersaulting him over the sides.
ARNO is on his knees – he begins to pray.)
Oh, Mary, Mother of Christ . . .
(*The horse rails back and forth causing the boat to dodge precariously on the stormfired sea. It's too much for* SEARLE *and* GRIFFIN, *both bury their heads between their knees. They don't care to look any further.*
The submarine fully passes them by. ARNO *glances up fearfully and is surprised to find himself all in one piece. But there is water washing in and out of the dinghy. There is an ominous gurgling of bubbles.*)
We're taking in water! God's teeth! We're sinking!
(*He reaches over and prods* SEARLE *sharply.* SEARLE *still has his head between his knees.*)
Bail, bugger you, bail!
(SEARLE *looks up tentatively. In front of them the submarine still holds its course, heading away. A fresh wash of water in its wake floods at their sides, drowning* ARNO.)
Oh, God, save me. Oh, God, save me. Oh, sweet Mary, Mother of Christ, not the bottomless ocean. I can't swim! I can't swim!
(*He halts for only a moment and stares with deep antagonism at the twitching animal in the bow.*)
It's that bloody horse – I told you, I told you . . .
(ARNO *and* GRIFFIN *set to, and a succession of objects rains out of the boat . . . a tin of gasoline . . . tins of sinkers . . . a small outboard motor. The first life jacket goes overboard from the frenzied hands of* ARNO . . .
In the meantime SEARLE, *feeling around on the floor of the dinghy, has realized that there is a hole the size of a fist letting in water. He frantically grabs at some cloth and stuffs the hole full of material.*
ARNO *throws away his second life jacket which floats away among bobbing bottles.* SEARLE *returns to bailing.*)
SEARLE: Was this in the dream – was it – ?
GRIFFIN: I don't know . . . I don't know . . .
(*The submarine now some distance away and submerging. There is a turbulence of broken water . . .*

GRIFFIN *watches intently. Beyond the submarine the city skyline is being revealed.*
As the sea beast submerges, the spear thrust of the cathedral soars into view.
Close in on GRIFFIN'*s face as he is thunderstruck by the realization that this is the same view he saw in the dream at the beginning.)*
Queenfish. . . !
(SEARLE *and* ARNO *watch it submerge (we zoom through it to the cathedral). They've seen the spire . . . but* GRIFFIN *is having another remembrance of the dream.)*

THE DREAM. NIGHT *(Colour)*
We again see GRIFFIN'*s dream . . . On the sea beneath a full moon, a glistening black shape, a sea beast, submerges into the water, beyond it the city skyline is partially revealed. As the beast sinks, the spear thrust of a cathedral soars into view. The medievals, now in their small boat, paddle towards it. . .*

We see figures running: SEARLE, MARTIN, ARNO *and* GRIFFIN *race towards the cathedral. . .*

CONNOR'*s distorted face screaming, screaming – he is clearly travelling at great speed on horse or wagon . . . water skims by in the background.*
The cathedral bell tolls once. . .

Hand over hand, one gloved, one not, the figure on the cathedral grasps for handholds . . . and misses . . . the figure perched on the spire starts to slip.
The cathedral bell tolls a second time. . .

The people on the ground race to catch the figure. Others race around and around the stone spiral stairs of the cathedral – but too late . . . the figure falls from the cathedral . . . as the bell chimes one third and final time. . .

And in the lake a coffin is pushed into the current . . . the dream starts to fade. . .

THE OCEAN. NIGHT (*Colour*)

GRIFFIN: I remember the Queenfish dive. Above it the church spire. One of us will fall. One of us – dead – (*Not wanting to believe what he is remembering*) One of us will die – at the cathedral.
(ARNO *closes his eyes – shakes his head . . .*
SEARLE *holds a grim silence for a few seconds – but this is clearly the last straw.*
Out of the silence:)
SEARLE: WHO – ?!
(GRIFFIN *is startled . . . he looks up at* SEARLE.)
(*Forcibly*) WHO – dies – at the – CATHEDRAL?!
GRIFFIN: I don't know . . .
SEARLE: (*Intense and abrupt*) No. . . ?
(GRIFFIN *suddenly realizes he's under challenge from* SEARLE. . . . *He switches his gaze to* ARNO, *and holds it there for a moment.*)
GRIFFIN: It's not Arno. (*Makes a hand-over-hand motion.*) Two hands – It was hand over hand before he fell . . .
(ARNO *parodies the hand over hand – one hand, one stump. He grins.*
But the elimination of ARNO *acts as a goad to* SEARLE'S *paranoia.*)
SEARLE: Damn you, Griffin.
(GRIFFIN *goes to move, but* SEARLE *blocks him with a swift motion of his leg.* GRIFFIN *looks up reluctantly.*)

(*Fierce*) When the die is cast – who is it then? Who will fall?
GRIFFIN: I . . . (*He was going to say 'don't know'.*)
SEARLE: Don't know! So you say. You can't see – or you won't . . .
(*There's heavy threat in* SEARLE's *voice, and* GRIFFIN *shrinks.*)
It's me, isn't it? The end for me. I've watched them all picked away. My wife in childbirth. The child she died for, picked away. My mother . . . picked away, picked away. Ulf – picked away and picked away . . .
(ARNO *lays a hand on* SEARLE's *shoulder, but he shrugs it away angrily.*)
No! He holds our fate in his hands, Arno!
(SEARLE *moves up on* GRIFFIN. *He puts his face just inches away from* GRIFFIN's.)
Oblivion, Griffin. I'm the last! I die, and my blood dies. My family shrinks . . . It's shrunk to nothing, nothing at all. Nothing!
(*He's shaking the boy.*)
Tell me! Let me save myself!
(GRIFFIN *wrenches free. He shouts back at* SEARLE.)
GRIFFIN: I'm telling the truth! I just don't know!
(*He stares at* SEARLE, *repelled and frightened by a grown man gripped by such fear.*)
It's not my idea! Why . . .
(*He stares at the rosary beads he's been pulling compulsively through his fingers.*)
It could be Connor . . .
(*He looks up at the threatening* SEARLE.)
It could be Martin – or you. It could be me . . .
(*He looks down at the rosary again and is suddenly no more than a small child.*)
I want Connor. I want my brother back . . .
SEARLE: (*Cynically*) Oh, he'll be safe. The luck's always been with Connor.
(GRIFFIN *has gone mute.*)
For the love of God, Griffin, tell us. We can't make a move until you tell us.
GRIFFIN: (*Stubbornly*) I want Connor. Connor would know what to do. Connor wouldn't be scared . . .

A RAILWAY YARD. NIGHT (*Colour*)

CONNOR *spins around as a powerful light bears down on him. A train comes screaming towards him. Caught off-guard he stares at it, not knowing which way to move – he turns in the opposite direction – no retreat there – a locomotive is steaming out of the yarding shed, and it looks to be coming straight for him.*
The train closer.
The locomotive closer.
CONNOR *is clearly caught in the middle . . . they are almost upon him, but he manages to back on to something large and stationary, just as the train passes and the locomotive veers off on to another track.*
CONNOR *has backed on to the front of a stationary train. It and the moving train are very close together, but the last carriage of the moving train finally clatters by. His eyes are rolled upward in fright, but as the threat passes, the breath of relief whistles out of him. His eyes thankfully close.*
Then he opens them and lets out an involuntary cry.
The locomotive he's climbed on to is itself moving, rapidly picking up speed.

THE BOAT AND TRAIN. NIGHT (*Colour*)

The train tracks run parallel to the water.
From the boat SEARLE, ARNO *and* GRIFFIN *see* CONNOR *on the front of the train as it speeds by in the distance.*
GRIFFIN: (*Yells*) Connor!!!

THE TRAIN. NIGHT (*Colour*)

CONNOR *is spreadeagled across the front of the engine clinging for all he is worth – his face is flattened and distorted, all the sound snatched away as he screams into the on-rushing wind.*
It's the same image GRIFFIN *remembered from his dream only now he can see that it's a train propelling* CONNOR *forward.*
The distorted face screaming, screaming . . . but also moving at great speed – we can see landscape, power poles, water, bushes . . . shooting by in the background . . . we can see the medievals in their

boat, out at sea – a flickering image, caught in fragments through the bows of trees. The moonlit water dancing . . .

THE BOAT. NIGHT (*Colour*)

The train, with CONNOR *its cargo, moves relentlessly towards the city, towards the skyline on which they can see the white spire of the cathedral.*
As GRIFFIN *and the other medievals watch he is carried further and further away.*
Then quite suddenly, GRIFFIN *looks away.*
GRIFFIN: Connor . . .
   (*He mutters.* GRIFFIN *is having another flash of dream.*)

THE DREAM. NIGHT/PRE-DAWN (*Colour*)

He sees a gloved hand reach for a rope. He sees figures running again up the cathedral stairs . . . the figure on the steeple hauls itself up hand over hand. One hand has a glove, the other doesn't as the figure pulls itself up the last steep bit. . . .

The figures keep racing up the stairs. . . .

The gloved hand reaching for the apex of the spire, groping – missing, starting to slip . . . the gloved hand trying to clutch the metal, missing . . .

THE BOAT. NIGHT (*Colour*)
GRIFFIN *comes back to himself with a start – he looks swiftly at* SEARLE *and* ARNO *– neither has gloves on –*
SEARLE: What – ? What is it – ?
GRIFFIN: None of us wears gauntlets . . . no . . . (*then he remembers – his hand flies to his face*) NO!

THE DREAM. NIGHT (*Colour*)

GRIFFIN *has another flash – of* CONNOR, *flicking the forelock out of* GRIFFIN's *own eyes with a gloved hand – saying*, 'Godspeed', *as he turns his back on them at the motorway* . . .

Again the gloved hand flails for a handhold on the spire, then slides helplessly, falling –

THE BOAT. NIGHT (*Colour*)

GRIFFIN: (*Aghast*) It's Connor – he's the one who falls –
(GRIFFIN *looks back to the shore where* . . .)

THE RAILWAY STATION. NIGHT (*Colour*)

The engine bears CONNOR *down towards a building – Wellington station. To* CONNOR *the building is just like a huge wall across the tracks, and he holds out a restraining hand in terror of being crushed by it.*
The train stops. CONNOR *comes off the front of it like a sprinter, over the buffer at the railway's end, up on to the platform and off, running strongly.*

CLOSER TO SHORE. NIGHT (*Colour*)

SEARLE *rows at full strength towards the city, but despite his best efforts, progress is slow.* GRIFFIN *is hysterical, pacing the boat.*
GRIFFIN: Connor's going to fall. He's going to fall. Connor's going to fall. Connor's going to fall . . .
SEARLE: Speak to him, Arno . . . And make sure he doesn't try swimming.
ARNO: (*Comfortingly*) As soon as we beach, Griffin, we'll run like the wind . . .
GRIFFIN: (*Distressed*) No, it's not fast enough! Let me take the horse – I've got to take the horse – !
(SEARLE *asserts his authority over the boy.*)

SEARLE: (*Shouting over his shoulder*) The horse stays with me.
GRIFFIN: (*Shouting back – hysterical*) Then I'll ride the huge sows – like Connor.
SEARLE: Stay away from those things. They're not God's work . . .
GRIFFIN: Searle, I've got to beat him to the church. Or he'll fall – Oh, bugger you!
  (GRIFFIN *rushes past* SEARLE, *stripping off his jacket as he goes – but* SEARLE *tags him and forcibly keeps him in the boat.*
  GRIFFIN *is kicking and biting as he attempts to free himself from* SEARLE *and pursue* CONNOR.)
SEARLE: (*Still holding* GRIFFIN) Now. You'll not leave us now. Will you?
  (GRIFFIN *nods slowly and reluctantly.* SEARLE *relaxes his grip with one hand, and with the other sits the boy down.*)

THE CATHEDRAL. NIGHT (*Colour*)
A short time later . . .
CONNOR *arrives at the cathedral.*
A rope drops suddenly and dangles in front of CONNOR *–* TOM'S *grinning face pokes out over the lower edge of the roof –*
TOM: Ah – right – you must be the man who knows about the rigging and the fancy footwork –
  (CONNOR *looks questioningly at* MARTIN, *who is working a friction winch, and already hoisting the spike.* MARTIN *nods, smiling.* CONNOR *looks back up at* TOM, *then takes the rope and begins to climb.*)

THE BOAT – CLOSE TO SHORE. NIGHT (*Colour*)
They're getting close to shore now. GRIFFIN *sits in a miserable little lump in the bow. He's running his hand over the cast-iron ball which is the boat's anchor weight.* SEARLE *shouts back over his shoulder . . .*
SEARLE: No one goes alone, Griffin. You're our eyes . . . You stay with us . . .
  (SEARLE *is bent over the oars.* ARNO *is staring towards the shore.*

In an instant, GRIFFIN *throws himself overboard, holding the cast-iron ball . . .)*

UNDERWATER. NIGHT (*Colour*)
Underwater he sinks like a stone.

THE BOAT – CLOSE TO SHORE. NIGHT (*Colour*)
Back on the boat.
The men are momentarily blank-faced in shock. ARNO *recovers first.*
ARNO: (*Totally at a loss*) Now what. . . ?
  (*But* SEARLE's *already moving, scrambling up on the horse.*)
SEARLE: He drowns and we're lost!! Help me! Hurry!
  (ARNO *rushes to assist him. Armed with the gaff pole,* SEARLE *leaps over the side on the horse. The boat rocks wildly as* ARNO *strains to steady it.*)

UNDERWATER. NIGHT (*Colour*)
Underwater, GRIFFIN *begins to walk towards shore on the bottom. He can see the horse's belly on the surface above him.*

BEACH – CITY. NIGHT (*Colour*)
GRIFFIN *reaches the shore.* SEARLE *and the horse are still in the water, but close behind.* ARNO *is further back, standing up in the back of the boat, and sculling in.*
GRIFFIN *runs up the steps to the beach roadway.*

BEACH ROADWAY – CITY. NIGHT (*Colour*)
A red trolley bus is pulling out of a bus-stop on the opposite side of the road.
The bus is already pulling away, but a latecomer runs alongside it, hitting it with her hand. The bus door opens, she jumps aboard, and the bus starts to speed up again.
GRIFFIN *looks back to see* SEARLE *spurring the horse towards him. He doesn't hesitate. He exactly copies the ritual he has just seen: he*

runs alongside the bus, thumps it with his fist, the bus slows, the door opens, and he jumps on.

BEACH – CITY. NIGHT (*Colour*)
ARNO *hastily beaches the boat, and sprints across the beach.*

BEACH ROADWAY – CITY. NIGHT (*Colour*)
SEARLE *rides towards the rear of the bus.*

BUS INTERIOR. NIGHT (*Colour*)
The BUS DRIVER *looks at* GRIFFIN *inquiringly, then jerks a thumb to indicate he should move down the back.*
BUS DRIVER: Go on.
   (*What strikes* GRIFFIN *is the formal layout of the bus interior. His only similar experience is the pews of a church. This impression is reinforced by the* FIVE NUNS *seated among the passengers. He goes down on one knee, and crosses himself. He bobs up to look for* SEARLE.)

BEACH ROADWAY – CITY. NIGHT (*Colour*)
SEARLE *urges the horse after the bus.*
ARNO *bursts out on the beach roadway, running, waving everyone desperately back to the fold.*
The bus accelerates smoothly away from SEARLE *and the horse. It vanishes around a corner ahead, and* SEARLE *wheels the horse down an entranceway which angles off in the same direction, hoping to find a shortcut.*

ROADWAY AND BUS DEPOT. NIGHT (*Colour*)
SEARLE *gallops straight into a depot. Suddenly he is in a place full of buses, but before the impact of that quite strikes home, he's riding at one of them, yelling.*
SEARLE: Gimme the boy! You took the boy!
   (*He thrusts his chin at the bus, jabs two fingers towards his eyes.*)

I *saw* you!
(*Then he sees this bus is the same as that one.*)
You! You?
(*He wheels the horse in a circle. Buses right round.* SEARLE *knows just how far he's out of his depth. He addresses the buses still, but those two fingers now point almost pathetically to his eyes. To his inability to see anything believable.*)
The boy. We're blind without Griffin . . .
(*Silence.* SEARLE *calls* . . .)
Griffin! Griffin!
(*Silence.*)
(*Quietly*) Gone . . .
(*In that instant of silence, all the loss, anguish, and uncertainty that* SEARLE *has ever experienced suddenly now wells overwhelmingly into one. A whimper escapes the dryness of his throat, becomes a second, and third, until it is a scream, a second scream, and a third* . . .
A bus trundles past the exit gates. With screams still bellowing SEARLE *rides like a demon to cut it off.*)

STREET – INNER CITY. NIGHT (*Colour*)

SEARLE *cuts through an alley and comes back out on the street. He's managed to get ahead of the bus, which is still several blocks back. With the hiss of released airbrakes it moves off from the corner towards him.*
SEARLE: (*Yelling*) Let the boy go!
(*There's no response . . . Only the bus moving smoothly closer. The horse spins and wheels under* SEARLE'S *nervous hand.*
SEARLE, *torn between worry for Griffin, fear, and rage, stares down the approaching bus.*)
Or we're done for –
(*With a cry he drops the gaff pole in front of him like a lance – and charges head on towards the bus.*
Sparks of blue lightning leap from the electrical hook-up at the top of the bus . . . it is transformed into something demonic.
The bus looms closer.
SEARLE *closer.*

The BUS DRIVER *blasts her horn in an attempt to clear the obstacle from her path . . .)*

STREET CLOSE BY – INNER CITY. NIGHT *(Colour)*
ARNO *runs at full tilt, getting closer to the scene of imminent confrontation.*

THE BUS. NIGHT *(Colour)*
Nothing the BUS DRIVER *does diminishes* SEARLE's *advance – when the bus swerves,* SEARLE *swerves, he's committed himself totally. The* BUS DRIVER *continuously sounds her horn – to no avail –*
The bus roars closer . . .
SEARLE *galloping hard . . .*
SEARLE: *(Screaming)* Grif-fin – !
  (The bus – close!
  ARNO *is now within sight of bus and horse.)*
ARNO: *(Gasping)* – God save us – !
  (The horse lunges ahead –
  The collision makes a tremendous KA-THUMP, the horse ducks out in time to avoid injury but SEARLE *goes straight through the front windscreen,* BUS DRIVER *and passengers screaming.*
  He's badly knocked on the head. He picks himself up, reeling slightly as he barges insanely past the passengers, smashing at one window after another in his attempt to escape. GRIFFIN *ducks away under this thrashing madman like everyone else.*
  Amid yelling and confusion, still gripped by a mad paroxysm of fear, SEARLE *bursts finally through the bus's rear side-door, and turns towards the front of the bus.*
  The horse gallops off down the road.
  The driver leans through the broken windscreen as the wild figure of SEARLE *reappears below her and begins to demolish the headlamps.)*
BUS DRIVER: Hey!
  (She sounds the horn. It stirs SEARLE *to a greater frenzy. The driver is on tiptoe leaning over her steering wheel. She sounds the horn again.)*

Hey, come on – that's enough . . . You'll hurt yourself!
(SEARLE *stops his attack. He turns, breathing hard, staggering slightly. There's a sparse half-circle of bystanders around him on the road now, and one tries cautiously to lay hands on him.* SEARLE *shakes loose. He turns to the onlookers.*)
SEARLE: Where's Griffin?!!
(GRIFFIN *slips out of the rear door. He uses the small crowd as cover, and peers out at* SEARLE.)
BUS DRIVER: (*Yelling to the roadside crowd*) Someone get an ambulance.
(ARNO *arrives. As he pushes through the people, he comes up behind* GRIFFIN. *He puts his hand on the boy's shoulder.* GRIFFIN *looks up – he accepts* ARNO. *The arrival of* ARNO, *however, has helped* SEARLE *pinpoint* GRIFFIN'*s vantage point.*)
SEARLE: (*To* GRIFFIN) We trusted you, and look where the hell you brought us!!
(SEARLE *advances, and* ARNO *puts out a restraining hand.*)
ARNO: Searle – please – we've got to find Connor . . .
(*But* SEARLE'*s too obsessed. He pushes* ARNO *aside. He advances on* GRIFFIN, *but the boy backs away. He turns and flees, burrowing himself in the crowd.* ARNO *is right behind* SEARLE.)
SEARLE: He's getting away – !
(GRIFFIN *bursts past the bystanders and tears away down the street – running blindly now, out of plain fear – he disappears around a far corner.*)

AN ARCADE. NIGHT (*Colour*)

GRIFFIN *runs full-tilt into an arcade, and stops dead.*
Before him, in a video shop, is a live television set.
Head and shoulders on the television screen is an American
SUBMARINE CAPTAIN, *wearing his cap, his braid. Behind him is the conning tower of the submarine, berthed at a wharf* . . .
SUBMARINE CAPTAIN: This is the real world 1989. You have an alliance with America. You can't isolate one little pocket of the world, and proclaim it nuclear-free. Because there is no pocket, no refuge, no escape from the real world. This ban they want . . . they're spitting against the wind.

(*For the moment of confrontation between the boy and the television, there's silence. It's as if the surprise of seeing a talking head in a box blows the words away.* GRIFFIN *presses his hand to the shop glass as he shouts at this person.*)
GRIFFIN: Where's the cathedral?

THE CATHEDRAL. NIGHT (*Colour*)

The moon, clearly headed towards dawn, hangs large in the background.
CONNOR *high up near the very top of the spire, hammers one last thing into place on the scaffolding. He freezes momentarily, hammer upraised.*
Far below, with a whinny and a clatter, the horse gallops into the cathedral grounds.
Seen from ground level, CONNOR *looks awkward and unbalanced. He finishes hammering the wedge into the scaffold.* CONNOR *is clinging with one hand to a rope, standing out from the cathedral roof.*

THE ARCADE. NIGHT (*Colour*)

SEARLE *and* ARNO *burst into the arcade at a run.*
SEARLE: Griffin – !
(GRIFFIN *turns to run, but is immediately halted by a rubbish truck which slides across the far end of the arcade.*
GRIFFIN *turns to face* SEARLE *and* ARNO *as they advance. He looks very small and helpless, framed alone against the rubbish truck.*
GRIFFIN *freezes up against the glass as* SEARLE *and* ARNO *advance.*
SEARLE *lunges for him, grabs him then suddenly stops in alarm. On the television set, behind where* GRIFFIN *stands, a sinister black shape rears on to the screen. The nuclear submarine slices through the ocean. A man in a rowboat tries to cross its bows.*
SEARLE *backs off – pushing* GRIFFIN *to safety behind him. A scream pierces the air, the death scream of a hawk as, on separate screens on other sets to their left, three identical hawks skim over the ground after three identical rabbits – hawks plunge*

– *talons hit* – *again the scream* – SEARLE *whirls around* –
ducks, and drops to the ground.)
(*Whispering*) There's devils . . . Griffin, the cathedral! The
refuge! Make us safe!
(*But* GRIFFIN *suddenly breaks down. He begins to cry.*)
GRIFFIN: (*Sobbing but trying to control himself, angrily*) I'm lost –
I can't see the spire any more – Connor – Connor's going to
fall –
(*In rage and frustration, he looks around. His eyes momentarily
scan the television with its submarine.*)
I don't recognize *any* of it!
(*The television shows the yachts straining to cross the submarine's
snout. Past rowboats and sails the submarine slides, black and
deadly.
The sight of the tough little kid in tears seems to have brought*
SEARLE *back to himself. He gets up and pulls* GRIFFIN *to his
feet.* ARNO *gets up as well.*)
SEARLE: (*Grim*) We'll find it.

THE CATHEDRAL. NIGHT (*Colour*)
CONNOR *clings more than half-way up the spire. His position is
precarious in the extreme. As in the dream, rudimentary scaffolding
has been erected at the top* . . .
CONNOR: (*Shouting down to* MARTIN) Get someone to sound the
bell, Martin . . . a signal to the others . . . The city's
vast . . .
(MARTIN *glances up from the winch – and hesitates . . .*)
MARTIN: (*Calling up*) Steady now . . . be careful . . . We've
still got some time left.
(*Not far from* MARTIN, *near the pick-up*, TOM *turns to*
SMITHY. SMITHY, *however, is already heading towards the
doorway.*)
TOM: Just a couple of pulls. I wouldn't want to bring the law
down on this little party.
(CONNOR's *expression is intense and driven as he works. He is
clearing the rope so the spike further down will remain unsnagged.
He turns and climbs the ladder to secure the rope. He's moving
fast – too fast for anyone's peace of mind. His foot slips off a*

rung suddenly, halting the rhythm of his climb. No matter – he keeps going . . .)

THE ARCADE. NIGHT (*Colour*)

GRIFFIN *looks up at* SEARLE, *tear-stained but gathering strength.*
SEARLE *looks back at him, gentle again, a leader.*
SEARLE: We're good enough, Griffin . . . to get there, and even if we're not . . . we must keep on trying . . .
(*On the television sets a yacht hoists its spinnaker. The gossamer fills with wind. At the end of the arcade, the rubbish truck has gone. They start off again,* SEARLE'*s arm around the boy.*)

INNER CITY STREET/ARCADE EXIT. PRE-DAWN (*Colour*)

The bell sounds once, faintly, but no one in the medieval trio responds to it.
They're almost to the end of the arcade, GRIFFIN *is talking to* SEARLE.
GRIFFIN: I'm still lost – it's like – I see too much.
(*They're at the end of the arcade, and the visual noise of the city opens up on them. Bright lights, flashing signs, in the big buildings, office lights which climb erratically into the sky.*
GRIFFIN *puts a hand to his eyes.*)
I've got to . . .
(*He was going to say 'concentrate'. Then he remembers the sound in the arcade.*)
Where?
(*But the bell is sourceless.*
GRIFFIN *swivels – he catches the first echo off the face of a smoked-glass high-rise. The bell's echo, the moon's reflection there – for an instant they seem like one thing. A false thing.*)
No!
(*He swivels the other way. He catches the second echo. And visual noise again. Signs, flashing lights, neons . . .*
A brilliant blue and white beam of light hits the bronze of the high-rise, shattering into blinding fragments. A police car, lights revolving, screams by.
Subliminal to GRIFFIN'*s stare, a blind man with dark goggles*

and a white stick stands beside a pillar.
But it's the visual confusion, and the city's noise which bears in on GRIFFIN *as the bell sound disappears, almost mockingly, into the city's background noise.*
Again, GRIFFIN's *hand goes to his eyes.)*
I've got to . . . Searle! Black my eyes – quick. Blindfold me!
(SEARLE *blindfolds* GRIFFIN. *The bell sounds again, sourceless, with echoes.)*
ARNO: Over there!
(ARNO *points, but* GRIFFIN *isn't moving.* GRIFFIN's *head tilts and swivels. Like a bat he tries to get a fix on the sound. Then he leads off in a direction entirely opposite to* ARNO's.)

ANOTHER STREET – INNER CITY. PRE-DAWN (*Colour*)

The bell sounds again. GRIFFIN *is leading the trio, tugging at Searle's clothes, and almost running despite the blindfold.*
GRIFFIN: Come on, come on . . . It's getting stronger.
  (*He stretches forward. He's like an antenna.*)
  (*Quietly*) Connor –

THE CATHEDRAL AND ENVIRONS. PRE-DAWN (*Colour*)

CONNOR *reaches out dangerously from his perch as the spike inches towards him . . .*
The rope quivers with strain, and unseen by anyone, one section of it is chafing, chafing . . .
TOM *is calling instructions with hand signals to* MARTIN *who's drawing rope through a friction-driven winch.*
TOM: OK! Right – slacken off a little! Just keep it riding there . . .
BOB: (*Grinning*) Riding high, eh? Something to stick right up 'em. Something a bit artistic . . . Something a bit bloody grand.
  (CONNOR *reaches out, hanging over empty space.*
  The medieval trio approach, GRIFFIN *in front, still blindfolded,* ARNO *and* SEARLE *behind him.* SEARLE *suddenly looks up. A shadow of fear passes across his face, and* GRIFFIN *senses it.*)
GRIFFIN: What? What's wrong?

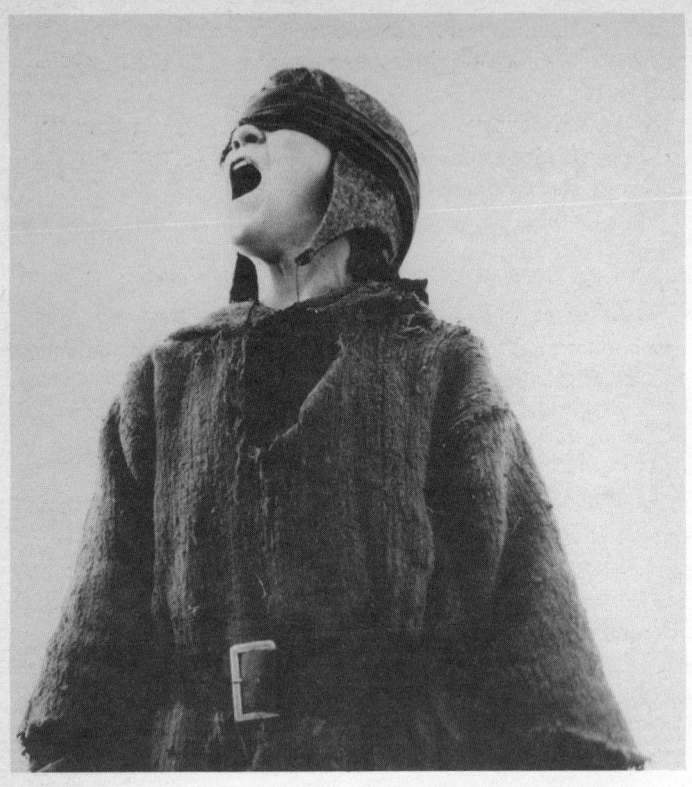

(SEARLE *moves up behind the boy. He puts a restraining arm across* GRIFFIN's *chest. With the other, he strips away the blindfold.*
GRIFFIN's *eyes are on the steeple even before the blindfold comes off.*)
Connor – ! Don't move – !
(CONNOR *twists towards the sound of* GRIFFIN's *cry. The turn, too rapid, affects his balance. He clings, endangered, as if about to fall* . . . GRIFFIN *breaks free of* SEARLE's *hold. He sprints the short distance to the cathedral door and disappears inside, closely followed by* SEARLE.
ARNO *rushes up to the point, just a few metres in from the winch, where the rope does a right-angle turn upwards through a snatch-block pulley. He looks fearfully upwards.*)

ARNO: (*Calling to* MARTIN) It's not safe for him!
MARTIN: It's all right! The winch is strong. The blacksmiths give good instructions.
ARNO: No. In Griffin's dream . . . In the dream, Connor fell.
(*The rope is chafing, chafing . . . The feet of* SEARLE *and* GRIFFIN *pound up the stairs.*)

THE BASE OF THE CATHEDRAL. PRE-DAWN (*Colour*)

The rope: beside Arno's boot, we see which part of the winch rope system is fraying. It's the guy rope holding the snatch block pulley in place. It's chafing against the stone at the base of the church but ARNO's *gaze is upwards and he doesn't see the danger. The rope frays . . . it breaks.*
ARNO: Jesus!
(*The heavy snatch block pulley catapults away from beside him, trailing its guy rope. The main rope springs outward – it slants straight up at an angle now. It's still intact, but the big pulley-block is now totally unsecured. It slides down the main rope, and is dragged against the friction drum. The big rope begins to smoke . . .*)
MARTIN: Quick!!!
(*It's an emergency, and his reactions are right.* MARTIN's *got to hold the rope ready, but the pulley-block is wobbling on the friction drum, jamming everything.*)
SMITHY: Look out! Keep the tension on – It's –
(*He sees the smoke.*)
TOM: Christ – it's jammed – it's burning! Grab it!!!
(*The rope parts but* SMITHY *has already launched himself at it. He's dragged sideways across the ground, then hoisted upwards.* MARTIN *flings himself off the winch and sprints for the trailing end of the rope.*)

THE CATHEDRAL SPIRE. PRE-DAWN (*Colour*)

With the slippage of the rope below, the spike falls. It drops on CONNOR *like a hammer. It hits him but he grabs it somehow, and he and the spike go screeching a short distance down the spire. As the spike shudders downward, bearing* CONNOR *with it, it strips away four or five rungs at the top of the ladder. He's bouncing and trouncing down the side of the steeple.*

THE BASE OF THE CATHEDRAL. PRE-DAWN (*Colour*)

MARTIN *lunges for the rope. He's dragged sideways along with* SMITHY *and up.*
MARTIN: Help!!!
   (ARNO *pounces on the rope out of nowhere. He's struggling to gain purchase too, when with a clatter and a snort the horse appears in front of him. Using its chest as a fulcrum he twists the rope round from stem to stern. The necessary counterweight to the spike is instantly there. More . . . the horse pulls, and draws the rope down easily.* MARTIN *and* SMITHY *drop a few feet back to the ground.*)

THE CATHEDRAL SPIRE. PRE-DAWN (*Colour*)

CONNOR's *dreadful slide stops, but he's left clinging to the spike with his feet thrashing for a foothold on the ladder. He succeeds only in dislodging another rung.*

INSIDE THE CATHEDRAL. PRE-DAWN (*Colour*)

The feet race up the stairwell. GRIFFIN *and* SEARLE *are neck and neck, but it's* SEARLE *whose height enables him to reach the trapdoor first. He butts it open.*

THE CATHEDRAL SPIRE AND BELOW. PRE-DAWN (*Colour*)

SEARLE *bursts through the trapdoor. He looks up, then swarms up the ladder. Twenty metres above him,* CONNOR *has lost his handhold on the spike. He starts to toboggan down the slide of the steeple, grabbing for the ladder, unable to reach it.*
CONNOR: No-o-o-o!!
   (SEARLE *looks up. He sees what's coming. He hunches, and bangs down a powerful arm across the path of* CONNOR's *slide. The impact is heavy. Another few rungs of the ladder give way beneath* SEARLE's *feet.* SEARLE *stops* CONNOR's *slide, and*

brings him to the safety of the ladder, but in doing so he himself loses balance.
SEARLE *slides down the fearful slope, without handhold. Jutting out near the steeple's base is a buttress.* SEARLE *flops across that, winded, horribly frightened, but safe.*
CONNOR *looks down the ladder. He sees* GRIFFIN *climbing resolutely up towards him.*)
Griffin! Stay back!
(*The boy keeps coming.*
CONNOR *begins to climb the ladder again. With some difficulty, he gets over the section immediately above him where* SEARLE'S *feet dislodged two rungs.* CONNOR *climbs. Beneath him,* GRIFFIN *climbs.*
GRIFFIN *reaches the first ruined section of the ladder. He manages to get over it, but his hand is bleeding heavily now.* CONNOR *reaches the top of the ladder. Above him, five or six rungs have been knocked away by his accident with the spike minutes previously.*
He needs to get across this second ruined section to reach the rope which dangles from the very top of the spire, but he can't do it. As he waits, GRIFFIN *reaches him, panting, bursting with his message.*)
GRIFFIN: Con – It's not safe for you!
CONNOR: It's safe for no one. The moon is setting. The spike's not raised . . . We've got to . . . Before dawn breaks . . .
(GRIFFIN *can clearly see the problem. Someone has to be lifted over the ruined section of the ladder, to grab the rope, to gain the boxing which surrounds the very apex of the steeple and guide the spike home. And there's no way* GRIFFIN *can lift* CONNOR, *so . . .*)
GRIFFIN: Lift me . . .
(CONNOR *stares at his brother. He's asking the silent question:* Can you do it? *And the answer that comes back in* GRIFFIN'S *gaze is:* Yes.
He takes off one of his gauntlets, and with his bare hand, he reaches forward to flick the forelock from GRIFFIN'S *brow. He stops short.*
GRIFFIN *doesn't pause. He begins to ascend past* CONNOR, *using* CONNOR'S *knee as a foothold. Then standing on his shoulder.*

He's almost past, when CONNOR *sees something.*)
CONNOR: You'll never grip the rope with that hand – here –
(CONNOR *holds up the gauntlet.* GRIFFIN's *injured hand is dangling down, and* CONNOR *fits the gauntlet on to it.*
GRIFFIN *brings his newly gauntleted hand up to grip the rope. For the first time we see two hands on the rope, one bare, the other gauntleted, exactly as* GRIFFIN *has foreseen in his dream. It's the first flash of the premonition, but it hasn't quite sunk home on* GRIFFIN. *Yet he senses something – something which accounts for the oddity of his final exchange with* CONNOR. *He looks down at his brother and . . .*)
GRIFFIN: Godspeed –
(GRIFFIN *starts to climb . . . As he does, his dream is played out in front of him as he's seen it so many times before: hand over hand, one gloved, one not, only this time the hand is smaller . . . a child's hand and it belongs to . . . it belongs to . . .*
CONNOR *throws his head back, squeezing his eyes shut, then opens them again.*
Down below, several police cars have arrived. Momentary noise and confusion as the cops figure out what is going on and head for the stairs inside the cathedral.
MARTIN *gives a desperate and pleading glance up at the moon. Beside him, the winch-rope is still taut.*)
MARTIN: (*Whispering*) Please, God . . . let us be in time . . .
(GRIFFIN's *body arches as he strains to drop the spike into place . . .*)

ABANDONED PIT – HILL NEAR TUNNEL ENTRANCE. PRE-DAWN (*Black and white*)

LINNET *hurries towards the tunnel entrance, with* CHRISSIE.
GRIFFIN's GIRLFRIEND *brings up the rear.*
CHRISSIE: We'll hear the bells loud and clear at dawn if they're still well in the village.
LINNET: And the dawn's coming – for good or ill.

THE CATHEDRAL. PRE-DAWN/DAWN (*Colour*)

GRIFFIN *strains at the spike . . . and it goes. The men below call and cheer.* GRIFFIN *stands beside the spike, his face turned upward*

to it in jubilation.
MARTIN *and* ARNO *stand beside the horse, from which the rope stretches upward.* ARNO *is stroking the horse as he stares upwards into the lightening sky. There are tears in his eyes.* MARTIN *is suffused with relief and joy. His hands have drifted up above his head. They frame the medievals' final triumph.*
SEARLE *is on the safety of a cornice. He's on his hands and knees, still high on the cathedral, but he raises a knotted fist, kisses it, and wags it upward towards* GRIFFIN. *It's a gesture of total support.*
CONNOR *looks up from his position on top of the ladder. The spike rides high, in place above him, and he raises two weary arms to clasp his hands above his head in the ancient gesture of triumph.*
CONNOR: (*Quiet*) Griffin –
(CONNOR's *head slumps forward on to his chest in a combination of fatigue and supreme thankfulness. His hands go slackly back to their hold on the ladder.*
Back on the ground, the crowd of onlookers is pointing and cheering. TOM *and* SMITHY *have joined* MARTIN.
GRIFFIN *looks up at the spike's sharp black incision on the lightening sky.*)

ABANDONED PIT – HILL NEAR TUNNEL ENTRANCE. DAWN
(*Black and white*)

Dawn breaks over the Cumbrian hills. The first rays light up the figures on the hilltop. There's the sound of a distant celebratory bell.
GRIFFIN'S GIRLFRIEND *is the first to respond.*
GRIFFIN'S GIRLFRIEND: The bells! The bells! The bells!
LINNET: The bells! They're safe!

CATHEDRAL SPIRE. DAWN (*Colour*)

The sun's rays hit the top of the spike. GRIFFIN *grins as he looks down, but the sun's rays seem perhaps to dazzle him, the cheering to confuse him. In that instant he understands. He recalls his ascent, hand over hand, one hand gloved, the other not* . . .
GRIFFIN *reaches to catch his balance with his injured hand. He can't do it. He starts to fall.*
All is exactly as it was in the dream, only this time we are able to see one more thing . . .

We are able to see his face.
He falls.
The glove floats in the air.

THE ABANDONED PIT. EARLY MORNING (*Black and white*)

The scream echoes over GRIFFIN's *face. It is lit by an oblique shaft of light. His eyes are open. He looks as if he has just uttered the last word of his story, very aware, but he doesn't know what comes next. His eyes rove, dwelling first on one of his listeners, then another. He is quite silent, but very watchful.*
LINNET's *voice floats down on the medieval group.*
LINNET: (*Over*) Connor! Griffin! Hallooo!!
  (CONNOR *cocks his ear to the voice.*)
CONNOR: Listen – It's Linnet!
LINNET: (*Over*) We're all well –
  (CONNOR *almost lunges at* GRIFFIN. *He takes him by the shoulders.*)
CONNOR: You hear that? Griffin! It could be we've done it. They're well!
  (GRIFFIN's *watchful trance is broken.* CONNOR *and* ARNO *bend over him. He looks up at* ARNO.)
ARNO: It's a sign – I'm sure it is.
CONNOR: A dream. You've had a wonderful dream, Griffin – a wonderful story.
  (GRIFFIN *grins. He starts to rise.*
  MARTIN *is still sitting down, still stunned. He spreads both hands, talks as if to himself.*)
MARTIN: It was – like a window opened . . .
  (*And* ULF *is seated – and glum.*)
ULF: So everyone reached the great church but me . . . I got stuck at the black highroad.
GRIFFIN: You didn't get stuck, Ulf – you went under it!

THE MOTORWAY. NIGHT (*Colour*)

Spoutlets of dirt fly up from the motorway. ULF *has dug himself a narrow trench which stretches almost all the way across the motorway. The dirt flies up at regular intervals. The top of* ULF's *head rises cautiously out of the trench – just enough that his eyes peer*

over the edge.
GRIFFIN: (*Over*) We were long gone by then, but you went forward . . .

HILLOCK ABOVE CITY. NIGHT (*Colour*)

ULF *is creeping forward, alone, scared as a rabbit out of its burrow.*
GRIFFIN: (*Over*) You showed the little Virgin the celestial city . . .
  (ULF *reaches a hillock where the city's light suddenly spills over. He reaches up like a soldier under fire. He presents the statuette, face forward, to the city.*)

THE ABANDONED PIT. EARLY MORNING (*Black and white*)

ULF *gets to his feet as his companions laugh and clap him on the back.*

The medievals scramble towards the tunnel mouth, but ULF *is still unsatisfied. He asks up at* GRIFFIN:
ULF: The little Virgin! Could we place her in the great church?
(*But* GRIFFIN's *face is set.*)
Perhaps . . . Do you think it's enough to have shown her the city?
GRIFFIN: That's enough.
ULF: I did that. I did that much!
(ULF's *joy returns. As he runs towards the cave entrance* ULF *bumps the rotting hub of the ancient drilling machine, collapsing it into dust.* CONNOR *watches it for a moment then turns away from it, back to* GRIFFIN.)
CONNOR: Just a dream, Griffin . . .
SEARLE: A vision of Hell . . .
CONNOR: But what a dream . . .
(GRIFFIN *ducks his head, smiling shyly.*
ULF *breasts the cave entrance, holding the statuette up to the rising sun, shouting . . .*)

ABANDONED PIT – ENTRANCE. EARLY MORNING (*Black and white*)
ULF *speeds past* LINNET, CHRISSIE, *and* GRIFFIN's GIRLFRIEND. LINNET *is on the edge of great joy as she looks back from* ULF's *charge to see . . .*
LINNET: Connor! You're safe! Oh!
(CONNOR *and* LINNET *embrace. She looks down at a grinning* GRIFFIN.)
– and Griffin, oh –

HILL ABOVE VILLAGE. EARLY MORNING (*Black and white*)
ULF *runs towards the village. All the fires are burning, and the villagers swarm up the hill towards him.* LINNET, CHRISSIE, GRIFFIN'S GIRLFRIEND, SEARLE, CONNOR *and* ARNO *are a few hundred metres behind* ULF.
The bell at the smelting ground is being rung furiously.
Villagers clap ULF *on the back. They swarm on up to greet the others. They whoop and cheer the returned travellers. They swing*

each other around.
VILLAGER 1: God's spared us all . . . The moon's already down and no one's fallen ill – no one.
VILLAGER 2: It's past the danger point.
VILLAGER 1: The village is saved! Saved!
SEARLE: (*Quietly*) The dream . . .
   (CONNOR *gives a little nod, so do* MARTIN, *and* ARNO.
   GRIFFIN *pitches into the dance. He strips off his shirt and twirls it around his head. He's dancing, then suddenly he's gasping for breath. For an instant he falters, almost losing his footing. His face is doused in sweat.* GRIFFIN *totters, and he puts a hand under his armpit. He feels the shapes like the little eggs. He's at a standstill, an odd expression on his face.*)

THE DREAM (*Colour*)
GRIFFIN *sees again the slap* CONNOR *gave him at the motorway and hears his voice: 'Stay away from me.'*

HILL ABOVE VILLAGE. EARLY MORNING (*Black and white*)
GRIFFIN: (*Whispered*) Plague . . .

FLASHBACK – THE PIT TOPS AND THE ROAD. DUSK (*Colour*)
In a flash GRIFFIN *sees* CONNOR'S *greeting at the beginning of the film. He remembers* CONNOR'S *cold breath hanging on the air.*

HILL ABOVE VILLAGE. EARLY MORNING (*Black and white*)
GRIFFIN: (*Again, to himself*) Plague . . .
   (*The energy of the dance still explodes around* GRIFFIN. *The joyous clusters of people around* MARTIN, SEARLE, ULF, *and* ARNO *are still there.*
   But GRIFFIN *looks past it all to the bottom of the hill, near the water's edge, where* CONNOR *and* LINNET *stand.*
   GRIFFIN *forces passage past villagers and mining debris as he*

descends the hill towards CONNOR.

CONNOR *sees* GRIFFIN *coming towards him.* GRIFFIN's *breath is illuminated in the cold air.* GRIFFIN *brushes past the dancers to stand in front of* CONNOR. *He tears* CONNOR's *shirt aside.* CONNOR *doesn't resist. Beneath the cloth are the unmistakable scars of the plague buboes.* GRIFFIN *backs away, staring at his brother.*)

You knew! You were sick all along, and you knew!
(CONNOR *can only stare.* LINNET *stays at his elbow.*)

CONNOR: Griffin, I –
(*The other miners have crowded in.*)

SEARLE: Are we lost? Do we all die, then?
(ULF *clutches the little Virgin tighter.*

GRIFFIN's *brother* LITTLE TOG *runs screaming down the beach. His breath too, is clear in the cold air.*)

LITTLE TOG: The plague! The plague's come over Griffin!
(GRIFFIN *shakes his head slowly.*)

GRIFFIN: No . . . it can't be, because – because in the dream – one died – only one . . .
(*He turns from* CONNOR, *but* CONNOR *moves close and puts a hand on his shoulder.* GRIFFIN *jerks away from his brother. Most of the villagers, meanwhile, are far above the village. They're ringing the bell enthusiastically, still oblivious to* GRIFFIN's *plight.*)

How could you've come back?

CONNOR: Griffin, I swear I didn't know the plague was upon me . . . Not until we were in the pit, and then I kept my distance . . .
(*He looks over at the friends he has been in the pit with.*)
. . . from all of you, I swear, and . . . I was afraid . . . There was nothing else I could do . . . you understand? There was nowhere else for me to go . . . and I came to believe the unfolding of Griffin's story was . . . I came to believe it was my salvation . . .
(*He looks around the still gathering circle of villagers.*)
. . . the salvation of us all . . .

GRIFFIN: But – the dream made you all safe . . . (*Wanting only one answer*) It's true isn't it?
(CONNOR *nods.*)

CONNOR: I think so . . . The plague has left me. I'm mended.
(GRIFFIN *nods*.)
All that remains – just a scar . . .
SEARLE: But – if the infection's loose!
(LINNET's *hand floats to her belly*.)
GRIFFIN: No! In the dream only one fell. I – it won't break loose –
(*He's enormously sad. But also enormously sure.*)
I'll not return to the village. I want them to know the threat is gone . . . the village safe . . .
(CONNOR *begins to protest, but is silenced as* GRIFFIN *continues*.)
(*Looking at* CONNOR) You'll tell them. You'll bring them round, make them believe my story. They must. You'll tell them . . . That's when they'll believe it.
(GRIFFIN *turns to stare out over the water. His eyes lose focus as he goes into the remainder of his final flashes of dream . . .*)

THE DREAM. DAWN (*Colour*)

Water . . . the lake. A box is being propelled through the water. It's a coffin, sealed, being pushed into the current.

LINNET *holds on to a rope as she squats on a pile of clean rags. Her face is beaded with sweat, her breath comes in fast shallow pants. The* GRANDMOTHER *is beside her, also the village* MIDWIFE. *The* MIDWIFE *hoists a* NEWBORN CHILD *aloft, umbilical cord still attached, and steaming with warmth in the winter's air.*
GRANDMOTHER: (*Mumbling*) A boy, a boy, a boy . . . by the life of me, a good fast birth. I'll fetch Connor, I'll fetch him . . .

THE LAKESIDE. EARLY MORNING (*Black and white*)

We return to GRIFFIN, *still dreaming, eyes staring vacantly out towards the lake. Those around him are silent, as once again we follow briefly through a further flash of dream . . .*

THE DREAM. DAWN (*Colour*)

Water . . . the lake. A box being propelled through the water. CONNOR *pushes the coffin through waist-deep water. We see* CONNOR'S *face as he pushes the coffin out into the current.*

THE LAKESIDE. EARLY MORNING (*Black and white*)

For an instant GRIFFIN *shakes himself from his dream and focuses on those around him.*
GRIFFIN: I'll not return to the village . . . I want them to know the threat is gone.
(*Then we see into* GRIFFIN'*s eyes again. They shift focus and drift, as he sees the final phase of the dream.*)

THE DREAM. DAWN (*Colour*)

SEARLE, MARTIN, ULF *and* ARNO *are standing in the background on a little rise by the shore, watching soberly as* CONNOR *pushes the*

coffin out until the current catches it. The men onshore are clustered together, saying farewell in their own way. Behind them, the GRANDMOTHER hobbles down from the village.
Close on CONNOR as he catches his balance from the push and straightens up. He watches the coffin float away.
The rosary beads nailed to the side of the coffin trail through the water.
CONNOR: Godspeed.